HUNTING

STATIC

JAYDE LAYNE

THE WHUMPY PRINTING PRESS

CONTENTS

— • —

Content Warnings

This story contains the following content:

- Monsters

- Death of parents and sibling (child death)

- implied/referenced child abuse

If this book isn't for you, no worries! But if it is, we hope you enjoy this story about a monster known as The Creech and the hunters who are trying to stop it...

1

STREETLIGHTS

After the bus drove away, the only sound was the crickets in the grass. It was almost eleven p.m., but the air in Tulsa was warm and balmy, decent enough to sleep at the bus station if she wanted to. She wasn't sure if she wanted to. After being on a cramped bus all day, she really didn't want to spend the night on a metal bench.

She slid her phone out of her pocket. The blue light was a stark contrast to the orange of the streetlights that stretched down the dark, desolate road, disappearing onto a black freeway in one direction and meeting the glitter of the city in the other. No one in Shadow Watch lived in Tulsa, if she remembered correctly, but it was worth checking anyway.

It took a moment for her data to connect this far from the city. She sighed, rolled her shoulders under her backpack, and moved to sit on one of the dusty benches. She might be willing to splurge on a motel room if she could find one within walking distance – her whole body ached for a mattress, even a shitty one.

Finally, her phone connected. There were a few people on-line, scattered as they were across time zones. Navigating to the 'Sanctuary' role, she scrolled through the list of users, checking the cities in their bios. Tucson, Santa Fe, Waco, El Paso, LA, San Francisco, San Diego, Seattle, Portland, Miami, DC, Raleigh, Atlanta, New Orleans, Chicago, Albany, Kansas City, Detroit – as expected, no one in Tulsa.

"Fuck," she muttered. She scrolled idly through the various chats, getting rid of notifications as she tried to make her tired brain think of what to do. In the general chat Sarah had been exchanging knitting patterns with MadHatter; Sarah had lost her husband several years ago to a chupacabra, but her bad hip kept her from hunting, so instead she opened her home in El Paso to other hunters passing through. MadHatter was a nurs-ing student in Albany who taught other hunters how to patch themselves up – they hadn't disclosed much of what brought them to Shadow Watch, just that it involved a vampire.

The other chats were the same as when she checked them a couple of hours ago – quiet. No new updates in the chats for vampires, werewolves, fairies, demons, angels, poltergeists (though she should probably go through that chat and her notebook again, brush up before the job she was scheduled to do).

Her thumb hovered over a chat near the bottom of the list. There hadn't been an update in that channel for months, and for good reason. The damn thing was so elusive, went underground for so long between attacks, and there were only a handful of others in the server who had even seen it. Only one other was hunting it like she was: Corpse Queen, who hadn't been online in weeks.

She shook her head. Now wasn't the time to go back down that rabbit hole. She needed to figure out what she was going to do for the night. Right as she was about to close the app, the circle by Corpse Queen's name turned green, and a message popped up at the top of her screen.

It happened again.

Her breath caught. Her fingers were already shaking as she typed back her bland response: *what.*

Three dots. 'Corpse Queen is typing.'

I saw it.

A second later:

Come to Tulsa.

She let out a strangled, slightly hysterical chuckle. What were the odds?

I'm already here. What's the address?

***

She splurged on a cab to take her to the motel. It was what she expected, a crappy place on the edge of town, like most of Shadow Watch's nomadic hunters preferred, herself included.

She climbed the rickety stairs to the second floor. As she passed door after door, she shoved her shaking hands into the pockets of her leather jacket. She'd never met Queen in person or even heard their voice. She had no idea what to expect, and if there was one thing she hated, it was being unprepared.

Room 216, the same gaudy orange as all the other doors in the lineup. Fluorescent lights buzzed over the doors of the outdoor hallway, little white moths fluttering around them. She watched them instead of the door as she raised her hand to knock. Her heartbeat thundered in her ears.

Shuffling on the other side of the door, the creaking of floorboards. There was a pause, probably as the person on the other side peered through the peephole, then the heavy sliding sound of locks before the door opened just enough for a face to peek around the edge.

It was a thin face, with a strong, curved nose and tightly pressed lips. Their hair was red and spiked, dyed yellow at the tips to look like flames, and a black ring went through one of their eyebrows. They dragged their eyes up and down over her, then asked in a husky voice, "CyberHex?"

Heart in her throat, all she could manage was a nod. They paused for a moment longer, then grunted and swung the door open wide, revealing the worn white tank top they wore and the splotch of red covering their left side.

"Come in, then."

Hex hurried inside and closed the door behind her. The room was like every other motel room she'd been in, except for the large military backpack sitting on the bed and the open first aid kit on the tiny side table. Questions itched at the back of her throat, but for the moment concern won out, and she swallowed them down. There would be time for questions later.

"It got you, huh?" she managed to say, and Queen shook their head as they eased themself onto the edge of the bed with a wince.

"Oh, yeah. Those claws you remember aren't just for show."

She cleared her throat. "Do you – want help?"

Queen grimaced again, as if they didn't like what they were about to say, but still answered, "Yeah, please. I can't quite reach all of it."

With a gulp, Hex set her backpack on the end of the bed. She didn't know a lot about medicine, but she knew how to stitch up a wound. Hopefully that would be enough.

Queen pulled the tank top over their head and dropped it to the floor. They had several scars from hunts and two matching ones under their pectorals, though Hex's eye was immediately drawn to the gouges running down their side, right under their shoulder. There were four of varying sizes, like bloody fingers.

"Shit."

Queen huffed, almost a laugh. "That was pretty much my reaction too."

Hex knelt down next to Queen's legs to get a better look. They weren't so bad up close – bloody as hell, but shallow, a glancing blow. She forced herself to breathe out and backed up to get the kit from the bedside table.

Using that as an excuse not to look at them, Hex asked, "So, um, what should I call you?"

"Cory," they answered quietly. "He."

"Okay." She returned to her previous position, ready to get down to business, only to notice Cory's raised eyebrow. "Oh, um, Hex is fine. She." Cory nodded and finally looked away, letting Hex focus on her task. "This is going to sting."

Cory didn't flinch as she cleaned away the blood. She could see his ribs move as his breath caught sometimes, but no other sound escaped him until he said, "Is it going to need stitches?"

"I mean, I'm not an authority, but I don't think so."

He let out a relieved breath. "Great. That would've hurt like a bitch."

Setting a bloodied alcohol wipe aside, Hex began ripping open packaging for gauze pads and medical tape. She should have waited until the first aid was done, but she couldn't resist anymore – she *had* to know.

"So ... what happened?"

Cory gave a tired sigh, but didn't rebuff her. "There's a suburb," he began, pausing for a wince as Hex taped down a pad. "On the other side of the city. Another family thought their neighbors were casting curses, so I went in to take a look around. Didn't find anything about magic, but when I was going through their basement, I heard static."

Chills rolled down Hex's arms and into her fingers.

"I checked for what could be causing it, but I couldn't find anything. So I said fuck the curses and hid in a closet to wait it out. I was right – a few hours later, the fog came in."

Hex forced herself to exhale. "Did it look the same?"

Cory nodded. His eyes were glazed as he stared at the floor, no longer reacting to Hex as she layered gauze on his wounds. "Yeah," he whispered. "That same gray light." He sat up straight and shook himself. "I followed the static upstairs. The couple who lived there had already gone to bed, and it was in their bedroom, just standing over them, like it was trying to decide which one of them to eat first."

Done with her first aid, Hex sat down beside him on the bed, hanging on his every word. The image in her mind's eye was crystal clear: the tall figure, skin all scribbled-in like a little kid's drawing. She was shaking – she hadn't stopped shaking since she got to the hotel room.

"What did you do?"

"Shot it." Cory dragged his bag over to him, trying to suppress the winces the motions caused. "With a .45. Didn't do anything."

"Didn't do anything?" Hex asked with a frown as Cory pulled on a new shirt. "What do you mean? Did it ricochet or go through it or ..."

"It took the hit, the bullet went in and left a black hole, but it didn't drop. Getting shot just pissed it off. It flashed across the room to me – you remember how it moves?"

Hex shuddered and nodded.

"I dodged, but it still got me a little." Cory reached around to pat the bandages under the new, clean shirt. "But here's where it gets weird. When I smacked into the wall, the spirit box I had in one of my pockets turned on. And I swear to God the thing *flinched*."

Hex's eyes widened. Before she could ask any questions, Cory continued, like he knew that if he let her start asking, she'd never stop.

"It looked at me, looked back at the people it was going to eat, and glitched out. Then the fog lifted and it was gone."

"Holy shit." Hex sat back, running her hands through her own badly dyed black and purple hair. This was the closest she'd gotten to it in twelve years – it had been here, in this city, only a few hours ago. So close, and yet. "What about the other people?"

Cory shrugged. "They still had their faces and were screaming their heads off, so I assumed they were fine and high-tailed it out of there. They'll probably remember it as an attempted robbery and tell themselves the monster they saw was a dream."

Hex's mind raced. There were a million things to check, a million details to examine. She had to get it all in order before her head exploded. "Okay, okay, let's start over."

Grabbing her bag from the foot of the bed, Hex flipped through the various notebooks until she found the oldest one, with its worn cover and duct-taped spine. Scrawled on it in permanent marker were the words, 'The Creech.'

"Wow," said Cory as she dug around for a pen. "I thought you were joking about the notebooks."

Notebook and pen in hand, she turned herself sideways and crossed her legs, not caring that her muddy boots were on the comforter. "Start from the beginning. What was the address?"

Bemused, Cory rattled it off. Hex put a star next to it on the page to remind herself to add it to her map later before moving on. The date matched – the last attack had been eight months ago, when the Creech took a ten-year-old, and the timeframe matched her estimates of how long it could go between victims.

"Who lived in the house? What were their names?"

"Just the two adults. Jessica and Brian Ramirez."

Hex scribbled them down and circled them. She'd need to do some digging, see if they matched the Creech's target pattern. It was likely, with them living in the suburbs, but it was always better to double-check. Underneath the names she started to write down Cory's account, but didn't get far before she felt his curious gaze burning into the top of her head and looked up.

"What? Why are you looking at me like that?"

Cory shook his head. "Nothing, I just – this is why I asked you to come. There's no folklore for this thing, nothing to fall back on, except for you. I knew you'd be able to put it all together. I'm more of a shoot first, ask questions later kind of guy."

"Yeah, well" – she spun her pen over her knuckles – "it's kind of my thing. When your spirit box turned on, did you see what frequency it was at?"

"Oh, uh, 103.9, I think?"

She wrote it down and circled it three times. If certain frequencies could hurt or deter it, they might be able to trap it.

Or kill it.

Going over the data again, a realization pushed the butterflies from her stomach to her throat, and Cory noticed.

"What?"

Her knuckles turned white around her pen. "You interrupted it. It didn't get to feed. It ran away. It's still hungry." She swallowed hard and lifted her eyes from the page. Cory's were burning brighter than his hair. "It's going to hunt again, soon."

Cory's smile was sharp. "Then so will we."

2

— · —

FOG LIGHTS

The light was wrong. She could tell even through her closed eyelids that there was something off about it. When she opened them and saw the gray, her first thought was that it was just weirdly cloudy outside. But that wouldn't explain why her dresser wasn't casting a shadow, or why the windowless hallway on the other side of her open bedroom door was as bright as her room.

She sat up in bed with a jaw-cracking yawn. It was Saturday morning. The last thing she wanted to be doing was getting up before noon, but the house was so quiet. Mason should've been pounding on her door by then, or racing up and down the hall like the Tasmanian devil while the voices of her mother and father drifted up the staircase from the kitchen. But there was nothing. Had they gone out without her?

She glanced at her alarm clock, but to her surprise, it was blank. Not flashing, like the power had gone out during the night, but blank, as though it wasn't plugged in, though she could see it was, and she couldn't hear the AC running. Maybe the power was still out?

Uneasiness coiled in her stomach as she climbed out of bed. It was probably nothing, but …

Her bedroom window didn't offer any answers. The whole neighborhood was shrouded in thick fog, shrinking the world down to just her yard, lined around the edges with the dark, eerie silhouettes of trees. No shadows were cast, and she couldn't find the sun, not even as a dim disk somewhere in the clouds. She turned from the window with a shudder.

"Mom? Dad?" The silence weighed down her words, turning them from a shout to a whisper, and she got no answer. She couldn't hear any cars passing by, though the road that went past their house was usually busy even on the weekends.

With a gulp, she moved towards her bedroom door.

All of the lights in the hall were out. She flicked the light switch a couple of times, but they remained dark, leaving only that weird gray.

Okay, so the power was out, and maybe her family was out too, or still asleep. There was no reason for her to be so nervous. Even if the fog was creepy. She would just go and see if her parents were still in bed, just to make sure.

Her parents' room was the next door down, which swung open soundlessly at the touch of her hand. The bay window across the room cast dim gray light onto the bed below to show the two shapes lying there, side by side, seemingly asleep. That was the confirmation she'd been looking for, so why did the butterflies in her stomach refuse to die?

Those butterflies drew her closer to the bed. Something about the stillness of the forms made her skin crawl – they were as still as the air, as the fog, as the light – she needed something to move. Something alive.

"Mom?" she said, reaching for her mother's shoulder.

There was no answer.

Her mother rolled onto her back as easily as the bedroom door had opened, without the slightest rustle of sheets.

She let out a strangled gasp and staggered back until she hit the wall. Fisting her shaking hands into her shirt, she whispered aloud, "This isn't real, this isn't real, I'm dreaming, I'm gonna wake up."

That was the only explanation for why her mother didn't have a face.

"I'm gonna wake up. I'm gonna wake up. Come on, come on, wake up." She couldn't tear her eyes away from her mother's face, where only smooth flesh remained, only shallow slopes where her eyes and nose should have been. There weren't even any veins showing through.

Over her mother's shoulder, her father's face was gone, too, including his usual scruffy stubble, leaving their bodies to stare at each other without eyes.

She wasn't waking up. Why wasn't she waking up?

Crackle. The sound drew her attention towards the hall – the first thing she'd heard outside of herself since she woke up.

Should she follow it? It might be dangerous, but this was a dream, wasn't it? Dream logic would say that if she played along, she'd wake up faster, right?

So she followed the fuzzy hum out of the bedroom and back into the hall. It sounded like radio static. Was the power back on?

It led her to her brother's room across from her own, growing in a quiet crescendo as she approached. Again the door was ever-so-slightly ajar, and the hinges were as silent as the rest of the house. She felt the butterflies again, crawling on the inside of her skin.

Something stood over her brother's bed. Not a someone – no person was tall enough to have to hunch in half lest their body go through the ceiling, with arms long enough for the knuckles to brush the carpet. It was impossibly thin, its pale skin filled in with black markings like scribbles, some floating outside the lines of its body. It was difficult to look at, the edges of its form flickering and jittering like a glitch on a computer screen.

Despite that, she felt a hint of relief upon seeing that her brother still had a face and was sleeping peacefully. That relief evaporated when the creature moved, reaching an arm towards Mason with long, wicked claws that hooked menacingly into her brother's shirt.

Slowly, the thing bent down, leaning closer, closer, closer to her brother's face.

Mason's eyes popped open. Staring directly into her eyes, both pairs the same shade of green, inherited from their grandfather, he said one word, so much more solemn than he'd ever sounded before.

"Natalie."

A creaking groan like rusty metal. Her brother's face began to blur, melting away like chalk in the rain, tiny particles of color drifting towards the creature's head.

Finally, she got the courage to scream. The sound pierced through the silence like shattering glass, but the creature didn't so much as twitch in response. All she could do was stand there and watch as her brother's face disappeared.

Mason's body dropped soundlessly to the mattress. The lifeless way he rolled, the blank space on the front of his head, made her want to retch.

She wasn't waking up. Even as the thing turned and fixed its pinpoint black eyes on her, she didn't wake up. The dread that had been building since she first saw the fog pushed against the back of her throat.

Maybe she wasn't going to wake up.

The creature jittered. A clawed hand moved in her direction, and it opened a maw full of sharp, strangely realistic teeth. Predator's teeth.

Something in her snapped. Adrenaline flashed through her veins, her skin went hot. Another scream scraped out of her throat, and she took off running down the hall.

The thing itself didn't make a noise. There was only the static, and a moment later a loud crash as it smashed a hallway table.

She nearly broke her neck going down the stairs before darting out into the living room, and knowing the doors would be locked, headed for the back. Her dad had always talked about nailing up the built-in dog door that came with the place, but had never gotten around to it, and now she was thanking her lucky stars for his procrastination.

As she turned the corner, she caught sight of the creature again. It wasn't running to chase her; instead, its flesh jittered within the contours of its body and it vanished into thin air, reappearing ten feet closer.

Well, she didn't have time to process that particular nugget of information. Instead, she focused on vaulting over the couch and scrambling through the dog door. The second she squeezed her skinny body through, she took off into the fog.

Soft grass tickled her bare feet. Outside the air was as suffocating as it had been inside, and nothing cast a shadow on the dew-wet grass. The fog itself was thick, more similar to smoke than mist, and the faint taste of ozone coated her tongue. Trying to ignore all of it, she headed for the barely visible silhouettes of the trees.

The static rose and fell behind her like the tide as the creature stuttered after her. She plunged into the tree line and kept going. She couldn't run forever, there was already a sharp stitch aching across her ribs, and she didn't know how far the fog went. But her only other choice would be to stop and bet that it was all actually a dream, and the longer she was wreathed in the fog, the more certain she felt that this was *not* a dream.

A shape in the fog caught her eye. She slid to a stop on the wet grass; the large oak tree with its many gnarls and branches like grasping hands loomed over her – their favorite climbing tree. The fog managed to make even its friendly presence seem ominous.

Shoving her bare fingers and toes into the familiar spots, she scaled the tree faster than she ever had before, going higher and higher until the branches were too weak to hold her weight. The bark scraped through her tank top when she put her back to the trunk, planting a hand over her mouth to smother her heavy breathing.

Not two seconds later the creature came into view. It glitched from tree to tree, pausing for a moment at each one before glitching to another, giving no indication that it was searching. It went right past her tree, and a few white-knuckled minutes later, vanished into the fog.

She waited until she could no longer hear the static. Only then did she climb down, breathing through her teeth to conceal the sound, and the second her toes hit the grass, she was running again, back towards her house. The stitch in her side burned with every breath, but she kept running. Maybe she could barricade herself inside – could that thing glitch through walls?

She only slowed when she reached her backyard. Her heart was pounding; she could hear it in her ears, feel it in her throat. Her side burned, her ankles itched from the grass, and sweat stuck in the inside of her elbows and knees. God, what was she supposed to do? Her parents were –

Crackle.

She froze.

Slowly, she looked over her shoulder. There the creature stood, jerking from side to side with that horrible toothy grin. Its flesh began to jitter, the scribbles of its skin shifting in a nauseating pattern.

She didn't have the breath to scream this time. She took off again, away from the house, and the static followed.

Where was she supposed to go? The fog seemed to stretch on forever. Were her neighbors gone too, already consumed by the creature? Was *everyone* –

Wait. There, to her left, a splotch of yellow. Yellow light, shining on a patch of grass. Sunlight?

She didn't have time to think about it. She turned, scrambling against the grass, and booked it for the light. From behind her came a loud burst of static, and the creature's claws caught in her hair with a jerk.

She threw herself to the ground and slid over the wet grass. Right into the sunbeam.

It felt like stepping through an old TV screen. It rippled over her skin, made all of the hairs along her arms stand on end, and there was a sharp stinging pain over her scalp as the strands of hair the creature had caught tore from her head.

Light. Bright, blinding light. She squeezed her eyes shut against it and laid there on the grass, panting. The static sound was gone, and the choking fog had disappeared, replaced by the warmth of the rising sun.

When she opened her eyes again, the world had gone back to normal. The sun was in the sky where it belonged, the fog was gone, shadows stretched over the ground, and birds twittered in the trees as though nothing had happened.

Relief flooded in so quickly she felt nauseous. It really had been a dream. There was no static, no taste of ozone in her mouth.

Slowly, she levered herself upright. It was crazy how far she had gone in her sleep and how vibrant the pain in her scalp and her side was, considering they were probably just remnants of her nightmare. Unless she had been sleep-running. If that was a thing.

She retraced her steps back to the house. A quick tug on the back door confirmed that it was, in fact, locked, so she crawled back in through the dog door. She must have done that in her sleep as well. She must have.

But the house was still so quiet ...

She shook it off. It was just a dream. It wasn't real. None of it was real. It couldn't be.

Then she reached the top of the stairs and her stomach twisted into knots. The table the creature had crashed into in her nightmare lay in pieces on the carpeted floor, mingled with shards of blue glass and trampled sunflowers – she could've been the one who broke it, she supposed, but wouldn't her parents have heard the noise?

She came to her parents' door first, and there was a second, smaller dose of relief when she pushed against it and the hinges squeaked.

The bed looked empty. For a moment that was reassuring – they might've just gone out without her – but when she drew closer, the relief evaporated as quickly as it manifested. There were no people in the bed, but peeking out from the covers was the collar of a shirt.

"Please," she whispered to the empty air as she reached out a shaking hand. She didn't know what she was asking for, but whatever it was, she didn't get it. When she pulled the covers back, she found two pairs of pajamas lying on the bed, empty.

She yanked her hand back as if burned, and without pausing to process, spun on her heel and fled back into the hallway.

Her brother's bedroom door was already open. Scored into the wood were four long claw marks.

A desperate sob stuck in her throat. She managed to keep it there until she tore the blanket off her brother's bed and saw his dinosaur pajamas laying there, empty. The T-Rex on the front was rumpled, looking up at her with pity.

The tears burst free as her knees hit the carpet.

It wasn't a nightmare. Why couldn't it have been a nightmare?

3

—·—

DAWN LIGHT

Dim orange light crawled between the blinds, casting alternating bars like tiger stripes across the page. Hex hissed a curse under her breath – she hadn't intended to stay up all night, but here she was, her phone at three percent battery and four energy drink cans scattered across the tiny table, courtesy of the vending machine outside.

She had accomplished a lot, though. She placed the suburb on her map, researched the two would-be victims, added the spirit box frequency to her hypotheses list, and updated the Creech chat in Shadow Watch with what they'd learned from Cory's encounter.

The man in question was sleeping restlessly on the lone motel bed. Even in sleep he had one arm wrapped around himself, like the pain from the claw wounds was seeping into his dreams.

With a tired sigh, Hex flipped back to her hypotheses list and stared at the lines. A lot of them had been crossed out over the years, those remaining more like genuine questions than hypotheses.

The oldest, circled and underlined so many times and in so many different colors of ink that it was hardly legible: *Why did I survive?*

Hex gnawed on the inside of her lip. The Creech had attacked numerous times, before and after Hex's personal tragedy, and she had cataloged as many as she could track down.

Only a third of those attacks included survivors. One of her old theories had been that it could keep people asleep, or at least docile, while it hunted, but if that were the case, there would never be any survivors. Unless it couldn't always control more than one person.

Another theory, however, could be that it couldn't affect people like that at all. It could be relying on the benefit of surprise, and people waking up in the middle of its attack was up to chance.

She wasn't sure which idea she preferred. The latter would make it easier to take down, certainly, but the idea that her survival was pure dumb luck made her stomach squirm.

Old mattress springs creaked. When she looked over at the bed, Cory had rolled onto his side and was rubbing his eyes with one hand, the spikes of his dyed hair flattened and disheveled.

"Morning," she said, and Cory jumped so hard he winced.

"Jesus," he grumbled, running a hand through his hair and making it stick up even more. "I forgot you were here."

"Sorry." Hex tapped her pen against the page. She should give it a rest for the day, close the notebook and nap for a few hours before she had to go to her job, but that question glared out at her from the paper, refusing to be pushed down for the hundredth time. Consumed by the thought, she didn't notice Cory frowning at her.

"Did you stay up all night?"

"Huh?" She looked up, processed, and continued, "Oh, yeah, guess so. Trying to put the pieces together."

Cory grimaced as he rose from the bed, but managed a few words through his ground teeth. "And did you – find anything?"

"A little." The rapid pen tapping continued. The pressure of her old, well-loved leather jacket kept her from resorting to bouncing her leg, but only just. All of these years later, the jacket still smelled like cigarettes and was still too big for her. "The city matches the pattern, and Jessica and Brian fit the Creech's menu. Good jobs, good lives, no evidence of addiction or problems with the law. Just a couple of parking tickets."

Shuffling across the room, Cory let himself drop into the chair across the table from Hex without answering. Despite sleeping, the bags under his eyes were bruise purple, and Hex frowned.

"Why did their neighbors think they were witches?"

Cory shrugged, then immediately looked like he regretted it. "The people who hired me live in the same cul-de-sac as they did. One of them didn't get a promotion they wanted, and the other's garden wasn't growing right, so I guess they didn't like the Ramirezs and blamed them. Like any other witch hunt in history."

"Hm." She sat back, her hands going to her jacket pockets. In one of them was the old knife. She wrapped her fingers around the hilt, seeking the reassurance of the comfortable grip.

"I honestly didn't think I would find anything. I figured if these people wanted to pay me to look around in their house and not take anything, I might as well, you know?"

Hex nodded and looked back down at the open notebook before her. That same question sat there, taunting. "We shouldn't go back during the day. If they called the cops, we don't want to be walking around a suburb looking the way we do."

"So we wait for night. Then what?"

"I'm not sure," Hex admitted, biting her lip. "I mean, this is new territory. As far as we know, it's never been interrupted and chased away without consuming at least one person. We can guess that it'll stay in the same general area and try to hunt again as soon as it can, but it's still just a guess."

"Yeah," sighed Cory. Folding his arms on the table, he rested his chin on them, despite the pain the wound must've caused in that position. For a few moments there was quiet, the only sound the roar of cars and trucks as they passed the motel outside. Through the walls a radio played in someone else's room, but it wasn't static. There were words, though too garbled for her to make out.

The question slipped out before she could stop it. "How did you survive?"

Cory's entire body stiffened, but Hex didn't retract the question. She had regurgitated her story dozens of times, on paper, in typed documents, in voice recordings, going over every detail again and again and again, compiling her research on top of it to see what fit and what didn't. The process never got easier, but it was necessary.

Cory, on the other hand, had been stingy with details, and before that was fine – she didn't expect everyone to cope the way she did. Now those details mattered.

"I ..." His fingers dug into his biceps. "I hid."

Hex waited, but Cory was silent, staring through the table like it wasn't there, stuck in a memory too long ignored. Keeping her movements slow, she slid a hand into his line of sight.

"Cory? Where did you hide?"

He closed his eyes, squeezing them shut tight like he didn't want to see what was in front of him.

"Under my bed," he answered in a whisper. "I was just a kid – eight years old, maybe. I woke up in the middle of the night when it should've been dark, but it wasn't. It was gray."

A shiver went down Hex's spine.

"I went looking for my mom. She was in the living room, and that *thing* was – " He stopped short of saying it, picking his head up from his arms and shaking it, as though the motion could make the memories go away. "But it didn't see me. So I ran back to my room and hid, and eventually the fog went away. But I didn't come out. I was too scared. I was under there for – God, hours, at least, until a neighbor came looking."

His eyes opened, staring directly into Hex's like he could see into her soul. "You know what they found in the living room."

Hex fidgeted, but didn't break eye contact when she nodded.

"Just empty clothes," he continued, and his eyes unfocused, glazing over. "Nothing missing, no sign of foul play. They made it a missing person's case that's probably still sitting in a filing cabinet somewhere."

The quiet returned. Hex let him have it, not saying anything until he blinked and zoned back into reality. He sat up straight, with only a little grimace, and squinted at her.

"How did *you* get away?"

Immediately, Hex folded her arms. It was a refuge, the black leather her armor, the knife in her pocket a sword. She felt like she was about to step onto a battlefield, but it was only fair. She had asked first.

"Pretty similar to you," she began with an embarrassing waver in her voice. "I woke up and everything was gray. When I went to my parents' room, they were already ..." The image floated before her eyes, faceless bodies that she should've known but were foreign without their features, and goosebumps spread down her arms. She swallowed. "Then I went to check on my little brother, and that's when I saw it. Consuming him."

She shook her head with a wry chuckle. "I was stupid and screamed. It turned and looked right at me. So I ran outside into the forest. I was able to hide for a while, but it found me."

Cory leaned forward, entirely focused on her. Hex held on to his gaze like it could anchor her here, in this shitty motel room, not lost in the fog and adrenaline rush.

"I thought it was going to catch me for sure. But there was a … I guess you could call it a weak spot in the fog, where sunlight was coming through. So I ran for that and kinda slipped out of the fog. Then it was all gone. All that was left was their clothes."

"You busted out?" Cory asked, eyes wide and voice awed. Hex shrugged, instinctively rolling her shoulders, trying to dispel the sensation of something right behind her, catching up.

"I guess? I don't know if I actually broke through or if there was a hole, but yeah. That's how I got out."

"Wow."

Hex took a subtle, centering breath. "Yeah. So, that's a thing. I don't know if that weakness is built into the fog or if it was just that one time, maybe it was hungry or something, I don't know."

Cory's eyes fell to the tabletop. His fingers tapped quickly across the surface to a rhythm. Thinking, but not talking, so Hex pushed herself to continue.

"And from you, we know that it can't necessarily sense people nearby. It can probably track by sound or sight like any creature, but it can't supernaturally tell where its next victim is, even in the fog."

"Or," Cory muttered in a dark tone, "I wasn't up to its standards."

"That's a possibility too," she said, narrowing her eyes at him. The Creech was a pretty picky eater – it usually went after middle to upper middle class families, ones that hadn't had too many negative life experiences. For Cory to not meet those requirements by age eight was ... concerning, and another discussion altogether. Not one for two people who just met in person, one of whom was injured and the other sleep-deprived. "A few answers, but even more questions."

"As usual," Cory snorted.

"Welcome to the life," Hex agreed.

The light through the blinds was growing steadily stronger, morphing from orange to the soft yellow of morning. Hex clenched her jaw to hold in a yawn – she would be crashing soon, no matter what her research brain said about it.

"I keep thinking about the fog," said Cory, still tapping the table. "What is it? A spell or something, or does it just follow this thing around?"

"I've thought about that. I talked to a guy from another online group, that Riddles in the Dark forum, and he floated the idea that it could be a pocket dimension. Maybe the Creech has specific requirements for feeding that can only be satisfied inside the pocket."

"Hm. It's as good a theory as any."

Hex sighed and unfolded her arms to rub her eyes. It was just past six a.m. according to her nearly deceased phone, and she was meeting her client at ten. There was time to steal a nap if Cory didn't want to immediately check out.

As though sensing her thoughts, Cory spoke up. "You should get some rest. Hunting this thing isn't going to be easy."

"I'm supposed to meet someone," she answered with a jaw-splitting yawn. "For a job. At ten."

"I can drive you."

"You have a car?"

Cory smirked at the obvious envy in Hex's voice. "Yeah. It's shitty, but it gets me where I need to go."

"Look at you," Hex teased. "Living the good life."

Cory chuckled, but quickly grew somber again. "So, are we doing this? In it together?"

"Yeah," said Hex. "Together."

4

—·—

FLASHLIGHTS

They pulled in to the suburb a couple of hours after sunset. Perfect cookie-cutter houses extended as far as the eye could see, a labyrinth of cul-de-sacs and sidewalks, lit with bright LED streetlights. Hex had lost count of the number of suburbs she'd been to, all across the country, but they all invariably looked and felt the same. There was variation in regional architecture, differences in the number of parks and the hue of the grass lawns, but all with the same restrictive, reverent hush, the same creeping sensation of being watched by unseen eyes, the same distant barking of dogs.

Hex took a deep, shaky breath. She'd been tracking this thing for years, but always a step behind. She'd never been so close.

Cory killed the engine on his shitty old pick-up and twisted around to grab something from his pack in the backseat. Hex unzipped her own backpack, sitting on the floor between her feet, and produced the same gadget she'd used in the haunted house earlier that day. It would need to be calibrated again before they could hunt.

"What's that for?" asked Cory, gesturing to the detector, and Hex raised an eyebrow.

"It detects radio waves. Haven't you hunted ghosts before?"

Cory scrunched up his nose. "I know what it *does*. But this thing isn't a ghost. So, what's the point?"

"The Creech gives off a signal," she explained as she fiddled with dials and buttons. "It's very specific, and it lasts for years." She'd broken into plenty of places – including her own childhood home – to prove it. "All of this is in the chat in Shadow Watch, you know."

Cory snorted and climbed out of the truck, Hex following a moment later.

"Shoot first and ask questions later, remember?"

"Still," Hex insisted as Cory came around to the sidewalk they were parked along. "I update it every time I find something new."

"And when was the last time that happened?"

The bitterness in his voice pulled her up short. Before she could decipher who that bitterness was aimed at, he came up alongside and nudged her shoulder. "Come on, brainiac. Let's get moving."

They set a quick pace down the street. They didn't want to linger in one place for too long; the neighborhood was fairly nice, and neither of them looked like they belonged, with Hex's ratty jeans and boots, oversized black leather jacket, and faded purple streaks in her hair, and Cory with his eyebrow piercing and flame-colored spikes. He'd donned a long, army green coat, very Constantine, and popped a handful of painkillers before they left for their mission.

Hex kept a sharp eye on the detector and an ear out for static, while Cory studied each house for fog.

After three or four blocks, Cory spoke up. "So, since I've clearly forgotten some important stuff, want to give me a refresher?"

Hex gave a hum of acknowledgement. "There's not a lot that will help us actually kill it, honestly."

The first mention she'd been able to find of it was in 1924, when a husband and wife vanished, leaving piles of clothing behind. Since then it occasionally popped up in newspaper articles in similar 'rapturing' stories, or accounts of people being found dead of animal attacks inside locked homes, or someone going 'mad' and babbling about a monster.

Going underground for months or years between feedings, it worked its way across the country at an excruciatingly slow pace, hitting any suburban neighborhood it could find. Based on that pattern, Hex had predicted it would appear somewhere in the southern Midwest, but with the sheer number of suburbs that seemed to surround every city, it was impossible to say exactly where or when.

That was the worst part. Never knowing where it was until it was too late. Cory interrupting it here was pure dumb luck, and there was no way in hell she was going to let the chance pass her by.

Cory kicked a rock, sending it clattering down the sidewalk ahead of them. "You said you talked to someone on Riddles in the Dark about it, right? Shadow Watch can't be the only group that's heard of it."

"We kind of are," Hex admitted. "I've found a couple of other people online and in person, but it goes so long between feedings that most people who survive slip through the cracks or convince themselves they made it up."

Or are threatened into keeping their mouths shut.

Her shoulders tensed at the thought. She rolled them under her backpack. Cory, with the insane number of pockets his coat and cargo pants had, didn't need his.

Cory took notice of the motion. "What? Did you pick up the frequency?"

"No, I just ..."

Should she tell him? They hadn't come after her in years, but they might if she and Cory started drawing attention to themselves, as they were sure to do prowling around a suburban neighborhood like this.

With a defeated sigh, she asked, "Have you ever heard of Project Chimaera?"

"No," Cory answered, kicking the same rock a few feet further. "What's their schtick?"

"They're basically the Men in Black. They work for the U.S. government. I don't know if part of their job is keeping monsters a secret, but it certainly seemed that way when I met them."

The rock skittered off the sidewalk and into the road. "You met the Men in Black?"

"Man and Woman in Black, technically."

Cory rolled his eyes. "Of course, my mistake. What'd they want?"

"Wanted me to shut up about the Creech." In her pocket her fist coiled tight around the hilt of her knife. Eleven years later and it still pissed her off. "Said if I didn't, they'd throw me in juvie with no way out."

With a shake of his head, Cory responded, "That's fucked up. But, hey, if the feds are killing monsters, it's a net positive, right?"

"It would be, if they were actually killing them. Some people have claimed to see them capturing monsters, but not killing them."

"For God's sake." He kicked another rock that was lying halfway out of its median. "I can't stand hunters who do that. Who cares how they work, they're dangerous and they need to be put down."

"I can see why people want to study them," Hex admitted. All of the windows on this street were dark, the residents all asleep, completely unaware of the danger that prowled in their midst. "Knowledge is useful. But when the U.S. government is doing it, you know that they're trying to figure out how to make ghost bombs or something."

As they walked, she never took her eyes off the frequency detector. Just as Cory opened his mouth to reply, it ticked over to a very familiar number. Hex stopped dead and threw out her free arm to stop him with her.

There it was. Static.

Cory's eyes widened in understanding. Slowly, they both turned to look at the house beside them.

It was the same as all the other houses in the neighborhood. White clapboards, basic roof with only a slight incline, the blue-trimmed windows dark, like eyes staring out at the street. There were two cars parked in the driveway, a truck and a Prius. On the back window of the latter was a sticker with four stick figures, two large and two small, and a little stick figure cat.

With a gulp, Hex dropped her arm and stepped towards the driveway. Cory followed.

Hex's heart was already pounding as they approached the front door. Cory tugged on the handle a couple of times and shook his head – locked. Hex glanced to either side, then tapped Cory's arm and pointed to the gate into the backyard. That one wasn't locked.

It was a well-manicured yard, with a big swath of grass and some neatly trimmed shrubberies and flower bushes. They walked across the grass, wary of the noise if they took the gravel path. Through the glass sliding door was a darkened kitchen; the gray light hadn't arrived yet, but as they approached the door and the static got louder, Hex had to fight to banish the memories from her mind. She wrapped her sweaty hands around the door handle and pulled, but like the front door, it remained stubbornly closed.

Cory tapped her shoulder, motioning with his head when she turned to look. Like most houses in the Midwest, there was a basement, with windows peeking out above ground level, just wide enough for someone their size to slip through. And, lo and behold, the first one Cory tested swung open on stiff, rusted hinges.

After shooting her an excited grin, Cory slid in with a dim *thump* when he hit the basement floor. Hex pulled her backpack off with shaking hands.

God, she hated this fear. She'd been looking for this monster for so long, and now that they finally had it cornered, that's when her brain decided to freak out?

Suck it up, she thought sternly to herself as she pushed her backpack through the window. *We're doing this, whether you like it or not.* Then, with only a moment more of hesitation, she went in after it.

She landed in the pitch darkness of the basement. Cory had already dug his flashlight out of his coat and was shining it around with interest, a thin silver beam in the gloom. The room was smaller than she expected, crowded with old cardboard boxes and broken furniture, with a rickety set of wooden stairs leading up to the rest of the house.

The static filled her ears. Biting her tongue, she dug through her bag until her fingers brushed the cool metal grip of her flashlight and the familiar corners of the spirit box. She pulled out both, but didn't turn the spirit box on quite yet, and left the frequency detector inside.

"When do you think it'll start?" Cory whispered as she shouldered her bag again and clicked on her flashlight.

"Probably not long," she replied, just as the room around them began to grow bright with gray light. She dragged in a strangled breath, tasting ozone – the fog was rising from the floor, pouring from the walls, curling around their legs, and the light was just like it was back then, just as *wrong*, the fog just as thick in her throat, and the static made it so hard to think –

Cory put a hand on her shoulder and made her jump. "Keep it together, Hex," he said, though it sounded like a reminder for both of them. His eyes darted around and his hand shook on her shoulder, but he was, for now, still calm. His fingers squeezed. "Find something different. Focus on that, not on the memories."

Hex forced a smooth-ish breath in and out. "The flashlights," she murmured. "The beams are different." They cut through the fog like silver roads, revealing some clutter in the room. It wasn't much, but it was enough to make her heart beat slower. She shook herself. "Come on, it'll be upstairs."

The wooden stair shifted at the first press of her boot. Hex cringed and froze, but any noise the board made had been swallowed by the fog. Cory prodded at her back, and she kept climbing.

Here the static was even louder. Without saying anything to each other, the two of them followed the sound further into the house, towards an open bedroom door.

The place was quaint, tastefully decorated, with a few too many crosses on the walls, but Hex barely noticed. Her vision was tunneled on their target. The closer they got, the louder her heart pounded in her ears.

When they reached the doorway, she pressed her back to the wall beside it, forcing another steadying breath, and locked eyes with Cory as she held up her spirit box. He nodded and pulled his from one of his many pockets. The static on the other side of the wall swelled.

Now or never.

Hex stepped around the doorframe and into the room.

And there it was. The Creech, standing at the foot of the bed, exactly the same as it had been more than a decade before with its hunched-over posture and scribbled-in skin. The edges of its silhouette flickered and fuzzed like a slowly dying TV set.

This time Hex didn't scream. Now, finally standing in the same room as the thing that had ruined her life, the fear was gone, replaced by a cold, deadly anger that kept her hands steady as she made sure her spirit box was on the right frequency. Clenching her jaw so hard that it ached, she pressed the button.

All Hex heard was a dull buzz under the crackling static of the Creech itself. But Cory was right – it *did* flinch, all the scribbles of its skin vibrating with agitation. It went blurry for half a second as it snapped around to face her. Those pinpoint eyes bored into her.

The Creech's victims, whoever they were, shifted under their sheets but didn't wake, not yet, and for a moment Hex was back in her little brother's room, his body falling lifelessly onto the mattress, until Cory moved in her periphery, dragging her back to reality – or whatever reality existed in the fog – as he flipped on his own spirit box.

To Hex's shock, the Creech recoiled from the second frequency, one of its spindly arms jerking up towards its face. The static pitched higher and dipped, a sound of pain.

It was working, the radios were actually having an effect on it, and Hex saw her opportunity.

Hex grabbed the dial on her spirit box and cranked the frequency up even higher. The Creech staggered, arms flailing, and this time there was something inside the static, something like a long, low groaning that the fog couldn't quite silence.

"Okay," Cory whispered in a hoarse, overwhelmed voice. One of the shapes on the bed shifted again, but neither of them paid attention. "Now you go left, and – "

But Hex wasn't done. High frequencies made it flinch – what would a low frequency do?

She spun the dial down, and immediately knew that she'd made a mistake.

In seconds the groan ceased, the static crackling high and sharp. The Creech glitched out of sight, into thin air, and before she could process that it had moved, a weight slammed into her.

She hit the floor hard. Her backpack provided a tiny bit of cushion, but it wasn't enough to stop her breath from being knocked out of her. Claws flashed overhead and Hex barely reacted quickly enough to roll away as they came down, embedding themselves into the wooden floor, sending splinters flying and a heavy vibration through the boards.

There was a flurry of startled motion and sheets and a high-pitched scream from the bed – they were out of time.

So far Hex had thought that only two sounds could get through the fog: voices and static. Now she learned that there was a third – gunshots. The shot ripped through the air, deafening even in the fog, and the static roared around them like a massive waterfall.

Whether the shot came from Cory or if the homeowner was packing heat, Hex couldn't tell, and it didn't matter. All that mattered was that the time it took for the Creech to glitch out and back in gave Hex the opportunity to crank the dial on her spirit box back up. The monster jerked and shuddered. Another shot went off, the muzzle flash bright against the gray.

Cory grabbed Hex by the arm and hauled her to her feet. "Let's get out of here!" he shouted over the continuing screams of one of the people in the bed, but Hex braced her feet when he tried to pull her away.

"No! It's right there, we – "

Bang!

The Creech's head jerked back as the bullet struck dead center.

But it didn't fall. It made an infuriated noise, an angry *hiss* that crept through the static like a snake through grass, and glitched out of the room.

Both of them froze. Hex held her breath, tension strung through every part of her, but the creature didn't reappear. Instead, the room began to darken as the fog faded, and both she and Cory hissed a curse at the same moment. The Creech was gone, leaving them in a room with a screaming woman in a lacy nightie and a man with a happy trigger finger.

Cory shoved her towards the door. "Run!"

This time she listened, scrambling to find the off switch on her spirit box as they bolted towards the front door. The floorboards vibrated beneath their feet as the man gave chase. He was yelling something, but Hex's ears were ringing too loudly to make out the words.

Cory made it to the door first and went for the lock. Hex glanced over her shoulder at the dark silhouette at the end of the hall; the arm moved, and Hex yanked Cory down just as the gun cracked again.

The glass on the front door exploded, raining shards down on their backs. An alarm started blaring, adding its high and tinny call to the tornado of conflicting sounds that were making Hex's head spin. Finally, Cory managed the chain on the door. He and Hex stumbled down the porch steps and took off across the lawn.

Up and down the street, windows were lighting up yellow, front doors cracking open, curious faces peeking out. Hex ducked her head to conceal her features and ran as fast as she could.

5

LAMPLIGHT

It seemed like only a few seconds passed before she was smacking into the side of Cory's truck, but it must've been longer judging by that familiar burning stitch in her side. The houses on this street were dark and quiet, so she tried not to close the door too hard when she climbed into the truck, slinging her backpack off of her shoulder and into the footwell.

The engine stuttered when Cory tried to turn it over. After three attempts, it came to life and Cory pulled away from the curb, shouting, "What the hell was that?"

Hex braced her hands against the dashboard and tried to breathe. The adrenaline still sang in her veins, she couldn't catch her breath, the fog and the light was everywhere, and still Cory was shouting.

"You could've gotten us killed!"

"Sorry," she croaked from a dry mouth. "Wanted to see – if all of them worked – "

Cory cursed and slammed his fist against the steering wheel, eyes wide and panicked. "That was not the time to be conducting a science experiment!"

Hex sat up and tried to lean back into her seat. Sharp pain pierced through the skin around her spine, sending her lurching forward again with a cry, and Cory's voice changed.

"Hex? Are you hit?"

He meant by the gun. "No," hissed Hex as warmth began to soak into her shirt. "Think there's glass in my shirt."

Oddly enough, the pain was grounding. Her thoughts cleared – there was something she was supposed to do when she panicked. Something with counting.

That was it. Counting and breathing. She inhaled as slowly as she could, counting to five, and let it out to the count of seven. It took several repetitions for her breathing to steady, and several more before she became aware of her surroundings: the black plastic dashboard, the AC turned up too high and blowing right in her face, highway signs flashing by the windows.

Cory was still babbling, a mix of curse words and assurances that she would be okay, that they'd get her fixed up, that they were safe now, and despite everything an amused smile curved her lips.

"I'm okay, Cory," she said, stopping the flood of words immediately. "Just hurts a little."

"A little? You were bent over for like ten minutes!"

"That was the panic attack, not the pain." She straightened up, not leaning back, and attempted a smile when Cory's eyes darted to her. "This is nothing. A poltergeist threw an entire standing mirror at me once."

"Jesus." Cory shook his head hard. "Okay. We'll be back at the motel in a few minutes. Christ, you scared me."

The rest of the trip was quiet, interrupted only by Hex's winces when she moved too fast. There was at least one bit of glass lodged in her back and more loose under her shirt, being pressed down by the weight of her jacket. She had about a minute to get anxious about possible damage to the coat before Cory pulled into the motel parking lot.

Cory offered her his arm when they reached the stairs, but Hex waved him off. Her knees may be shaky from the adrenaline rush, but her legs worked fine, and thankfully Cory accepted that without a fuss.

After all the chaos, the dark, quiet interior of the motel room was bliss. Cory left his pack by the door and moved to the center of the room, retrieving the first aid kit from where they'd left it the night before and clicking on the bedside lamp, filling the space with soft yellow. Her shoulders lost some tension – it wasn't the eerie gray light of the fog.

"Come here," Cory said, gesturing to the bed. "Let me look."

Hex shuffled over and slowly sat down on the edge of the mattress. The adrenaline was completely gone and for once she actually wanted to sleep, but that wouldn't be happening for a while yet.

She jolted when hands suddenly landed on her shoulders.

"Just me," said Cory. He pulled the jacket down and off of her with quick, efficient movements.

Once Hex swallowed her heart back down where it was supposed to be, she managed to ask, "Is it torn?"

There was some rustling and two *plops* as Cory tossed both of their coats onto the bed beside her. Maybe she was imagining how the leather cracked like a whip and the polyester snapped with suppressed tension. The tension in his voice was definitely not her imagination when he said shortly, "Looks fine to me."

Hex let out a breath of momentary relief, only for it to catch when the mattress dipped behind her.

"Need help with your shirt?"

Her throat was too tight to answer. She shook her head and reached for the hem herself; the shirt was a size too big for her, which made it easier to wrestle off, but the movement made the glass shift and catch against her skin.

A cursory examination showed that the shirt was bloody but untorn. A blessing – she only owned four shirts.

"Good thing I only wear black," she mumbled, getting a half-amused chuckle from Cory. There was a click from behind her when he opened the first aid kit, and Hex barely restrained herself from twisting around to keep her eyes on him.

It's just Cory. He might be a little pissed, but it's still him. You're fine.

With a hard swallow, she asked, "Do I need to take my binder off?"

Cory hummed, the mattress dipping again as he leaned in. "I don't think so. There's just some glass dust on it." A hand brushed briskly over her back. Hex clenched her teeth and her fists around the shirt in her hands, willing all of her muscles not to move as chills shot down her spine and rippled across her skin.

Cory brushed the back of the binder twice more. "There, I think I got it all. You have some cuts below it and a piece stuck near your neck."

Hex forced her breath through her teeth. The sooner this was done, the sooner they could figure out their plan B. "Just get it over with."

"Alright, give me a sec."

Hex braced herself. It wasn't the pain she was worried about, she could handle pain. It was the proximity, knowing someone was behind her and had the advantage. She couldn't see what they were doing or how much it would hurt and knew that it would be so, so easy for them to plant a hand between her shoulder blades and push her down –

There was a slight, sharp pain, then, "Got it."

Her knuckles were white where they gripped the blood-stained shirt. She knew what was coming next, but she still jumped when the cold antiseptic wipe hit her skin. Cory worked quickly, at least, mopping up the blood and cleaning up the wound, and Hex kept it together surprisingly well, even when she felt the press of his fingers as he stuck a bandage to her skin. Her hands were shaking and she was covered in cold sweat, but she held it together.

Then the wipe returned, this time in the middle of her spine beneath the binder, and before she knew it, she was three steps away from the bed, clutching the shirt to her chest as she shook.

Her chest was heavy. She pressed her forehead to the rough texture of the motel wallpaper and tried to slow her breath, with mixed results.

"Hex?"

She jolted, then immediately scolded herself. *Come on, Hex, pull it together.*

"Sorry," she managed to say in a semi-steady voice. "I just – I just need a minute."

"Did I do something?"

Hex shook her head without turning from the wall. "No, it's not you. I – I'm not – " God, she was so exposed without her jacket, without the baggy shirt to conceal the shape of her body. She couldn't remember the last time she'd let anyone touch her this much, with or without the heavy leather barrier. "I'm not used to this. I'm jumpy."

"Okay." Cory's voice was softer than it was before, so soft it made Hex's chest ache. That could've also been the hyperventilating, though.

He waited patiently for several minutes while Hex tried to pull herself together. Part of her was tempted to say screw it to the bandages and let them heal on their own, but the dripping of blood down the small of her back begged otherwise.

Eventually, she managed to step away from the wall and turn back to face Cory. He was watching her, a blank expression on his face that made more anxiety begin to twist in Hex's stomach, but for now he didn't scold her for making everything so difficult. He waited for her to come back to her previous position, and didn't say anything when she gave a too-obvious shiver at the chills that returned when she turned her back to him.

"Where did you get your jacket?"

All Hex could think to say was a puzzled, "Huh?"

"Your jacket," Cory repeated firmly. Hex jumped at the momentary touch of another wipe, gone as quickly as it came. "Where'd you get it? Tell me."

Oh. He was trying to distract her. Well, she didn't have any better ideas. Might as well play along.

"My third foster home," she murmured. A bandage wrapper crinkled and she tensed in anticipation, but Cory didn't touch her.

He just said, "Go on."

Hex gulped and continued. "The couple running it were taking care of the husband's father. Old guy, Vietnam vet and everything."

Cory stuck on the bandage at the end of her sentence, lightning quick, and Hex stuttered for a second. But only for a second.

"He mostly kept to himself. He had a bad leg so he didn't leave his room much. But he had a whole bunch of old stuff in there, including my knife." The knife that was currently unreachable in her jacket pocket.

Another cold swipe of antiseptic, another bandage, but neither were what made her throat tighten.

"One day, I snuck in there while the adults were taking him to a doctor's appointment. I don't know why, but I took the knife off his dresser."

That was a lie. She knew exactly why she took it.

"It was stupid and obvious, but he never said anything about it. One time, he invited me into his room and I thought for sure … but he didn't. He just asked if I'd play checkers with him."

The low lamplight of the motel room was so similar to the lamplight in his room as the two of them played, moving their pieces across the board without a word between them.

Another bandage. Hex barely noticed.

"Eventually, the couple decided to stop fostering. He needed more care, and their careers were taking off. So they sent me back." She couldn't quite keep the bitterness out of her voice. It was the same old story, over and over. Even in the decent homes, she was the weak link. The thing that could be easily discarded.

"The day I left, I tried to give the knife back to him. He told me to keep it." She could still feel the rough texture of his hands as he pressed her fingers around the hilt. His rickety voice when he said she needed it more than he did. "Then he gave me his old jacket too. Said he never wore it anymore."

The last bandage went on just in time for the crinkling of the wrapper to conceal Hex's sniffle – she hoped.

"All done," Cory said quietly, and the mattress shifted as he moved back from her.

Hex practically leapt up from the bed. Without looking at Cory, she made a beeline to her backpack to dig out a new shirt. It was just as big as the last one, a black concert tee she'd gotten from her dad, worn soft with age.

Her breath was still shuddering, and at the thought of her dad, her eyes pricked with humiliating tears. She had gone down too many memory lanes tonight. Clutching both of her shirts to her chest, she beat a hasty retreat to the tiny bathroom.

Click went the lock, and for a moment Hex leaned back against the door, using the pressure on the cuts to drag her back into reality.

Surprisingly, once the tears subsided, she didn't feel as shitty as she expected to. The chills were gone, leaving only the drying sweat to mark them, and she pulled the clean shirt on with a sigh of relief – safe at last.

Hex studied her reflection as the sink filled with cold water. Maybe it was the harsh bathroom light or the cloudy mirror, but she looked pale, sick, the bags under her eyes nearly the same shade as the streaks in her messy hair. Hair that needed re-dying, judging by the lines of brown at her roots. She shook it out to make sure there was no glass lingering, and when the basin was full, dunked her bloodstained shirt inside to soak.

By the time she opened the bathroom door, she felt fairly composed. Cory was still on the bed, one hand holding up his tank top as he inspected the bandages on his side. Bandages blooming with fresh red.

"Shit," Hex hissed.

Cory gave her a half-smile, tight with concealed pain. "All the running got the blood pumping again, I guess."

"Why didn't you say anything?" She was already halfway across the room, going for the first aid kit, and Cory didn't stop her when she dropped to the floor next to her bed.

"We were a little busy, and you had glass stuck in you."

Hex pressed her lips into a thin line and batted one of his hands out of the way. As gently as she could, she lifted the bandage away; the wounds beneath were irritated, red around the edges, and sluggishly oozing blood, but to Hex's relief, they didn't look like they were getting infected.

"Not infected," she said, and some of the tension in Cory's body loosened. "Just irritated by the running, like you said. Let me get another bandage."

Cory didn't argue, and said nothing as Hex changed the bandage, but his shallow breathing and trembling gave him away.

"Do you want pain meds? I think there's some in the kit."

"Nah." His voice was breathy, exhausted. "Don't wanna be knocked out if something happens."

"Okay." Hex sat back, letting Cory's shirt fall back over the fresh bandage. Wounds tended to, now would be the time to go over what happened in that house, get the data down, but the thought of it made her stomach twist. There was no avoiding it: she had fucked up, and it nearly got them killed. "Look, about what happened – "

"We'll talk about it later," Cory interrupted. The edge had returned to his voice, but the glow of the lamp softened the hard planes of his face into something almost child-like. "We need to rest."

"Right." Of course Cory needed to sleep. "I'll get started putting that house on my map and writing down what we found out so we can talk it over in the morning." And Hex could apologize.

She stood up, about to go negotiate with the vending machine for more caffeine, when Cory caught her wrist.

"Hey, I said we. As in both of us."

Hex balked. She was tired, sure, but she was used to it. There were more important things to do. "But – "

"No buts. You didn't sleep last night."

"I slept this morning, remember?" She tugged her arm away from Cory's grasp, but his intent stare kept her pinned in place.

"You napped for two hours. That's not nearly enough, and you'll probably be able to think more clearly if you sleep before going over everything."

Something itched under her skin. It was a familiar itch, the buzz of *go go go now now now* that had kept her up the previous night, desperate to sort it all out as quickly as possible so that she could move on to the next clue, the next crumb of information, the next data point.

"We'll probably only have one more shot at this," she attempted. "We need to know everything we can."

Cory snorted at her and slowly stretched himself out on the bed, wincing as the movement pulled on his wound. "You'll be useless to me on a hunt if you're sleep-deprived."

She eyed the other side of the bed warily. Cory raised an eyebrow.

"If you keep fighting me on this, I'll be forced to stake you."

That got a laugh out of her, and some of the tension eased. Enough for her to recognize the validity of Cory's argument, even if sleeping didn't usually go well for her.

"Okay, okay, fine. You're probably right."

"Come on then." Cory patted the other side of the bed with a lopsided smile. "I don't bite."

"I might," replied Hex, only half joking, but Cory just laughed.

Okay, I can do this. She couldn't remember the last time she shared a bed with someone, but it would be fine. It didn't have to be a big deal. So long as she didn't make it one.

Before she could psych herself out, Hex went around to the other side of the bed and climbed on; jeans, boots, and all. For a second she panicked over which way to face – *facing Cory would be awkward but facing away would leave her vulnerable* – until she settled for laying on her back and staring straight up at the ceiling, letting the sting of the cuts distract her.

To her relief, Cory didn't call attention to how weird she was being. The lamp clicked off, plunging the room into darkness.

"Goodnight, Hex."

She squeezed her eyes shut and didn't answer.

6

FLUORESCENT LIGHTS

"Natalie?"

Hex warily looked up from her notebook. It had been more than a year, but that name still left a bad taste at the back of her mouth. The feeling wasn't assuaged by the sight of a red-jacketed school security guard standing in the doorway. He gestured to her, and she reluctantly got up from her desk as the beginnings of anxiety stirred in her stomach.

The last time she'd been called out of class, it was to be chewed out by the principal for stealing (which she totally did not do ... this time), so she wasn't looking forward to whatever new lecture awaited her.

The security guard didn't try to talk to her. They never did – all security did was stand around in the halls, scowl at students, and buy weed off the senior dealers. He just led her down the many halls and staircases it took to reach the main office.

Then he did something surprising. Instead of taking her to the principal's office, he opened a door to an empty room, holding only a table and three chairs.

"Wait here," he said roughly. "They'll be here in a few minutes."

"Who's they?" Hex demanded, but he merely glared at her. So, with great reluctance, she stepped inside. The door closed behind her, and she heard the lock click. Dammit.

With no other option, she sat down in the lone chair on one side of the table. The room was silent except for the buzz of the fluorescent lighting embedded in the ceiling, so much like radio static. She dug her headphones out from her bag and put them in – she didn't play anything, she wanted to hear when whoever it was came for her, but they were enough to muffle the buzzing.

Then all she could do was wait. She'd gotten used to waiting – social workers were incredibly busy, and waiting in various offices had become a fact of life.

The room wasn't anything special. It had the same short blue carpet as the rest of the office areas at the school, with the same yellow wood paneling on the walls. One thing she did notice, however, was the lack of the red recording light on the camera tucked into a ceiling corner. Just as she noticed, she heard dim footsteps, and the door opened.

On the other side were two adults in black suits, a man and a woman. They looked like FBI, with the man's perfectly military haircut and the woman's tight bun, but there were no badges or identification anywhere on them. They came in and sat down, stiff and proper, and the man tucked his briefcase under his chair as Hex pulled the earbuds from her ears.

"Hello, Hex," the woman said in a saccharine voice. It was meant to be friendly, she was sure, but still she felt her shoulders tense. It sounded wrong coming from these people, the woman with perfectly plucked eyebrows and the man compulsively smoothing his tie.

These weren't school officials or social workers. So, who were they, and what did they want from her?

"Who are you?" she asked again, and this time got an answer.

"We represent the United States government," said the man with a smile that was too wide. "A small branch, but an important one."

He didn't say which, and Hex got the feeling he wouldn't if she asked. So her next question was, "What do you want?"

The woman cleared her throat and sat forward, resting her interlaced hands on the table. Hex leaned back in her chair, wanting to be as far away from this strange, perfect-looking woman as she could be. "We'd like to speak to you about your family. What happened to them."

Hex's stomach dropped like she was sitting in the Tower of Terror rather than a normal plastic chair. The missing persons cases for her mother, father, and brother were technically active but had gone cold months ago (because they weren't missing, they were *dead,* and Hex had seen them die). Did these people think they found some evidence? Or … if they were part of a secret government agency … did they know about the Creech?

Still, she was cautious. Three foster homes had taught her that. She narrowed her eyes and said, "What about them?"

"It's come to our attention," the man said, "that you believe they were killed by a supernatural creature of some sort."

All of her muscles tensed. Yes, she had told the police what happened, as well as her court-issued therapist and a couple of kids at school who had pushed her, but how did that get all the way up to the feds?

"So? Can't a crazy girl have her delusions?"

The woman's smile grew, straining at the edges of her mouth. "You don't really believe it was a delusion, Hex. We both know that."

Hex snorted and tossed her head. "Isn't that how delusions work?"

The man sighed, exasperated, but that was the exact opposite of Hex's problem. "The thing is, *Natalie*" – ah, there it was – "that we can't have you running around spreading rumors about a soul-eating monster. You could instill a culture of fear in this community, and that wouldn't help anyone, including the police who are trying to find your family."

"What?" She couldn't help her disbelieving chuckle. "No one actually believes me. They all think I'm crazy. No one's afraid."

"All it takes is one person," the woman said. "Next thing you know, we have mass hysteria on our hands, and that gets incredibly messy." She was still smiling. Didn't her face hurt?

The man was smiling too, but not as ferociously as the woman. "Whether or not you think people believe you, we need you to stop telling that story."

"Stop telling the truth, you mean," Hex snapped back. "Screw you. I have freedom of speech, don't I?"

The man leaned back and folded his arms. "Of course. Just not about this." He smiled wider, flashing his painfully white teeth. "We have different rules than most agencies."

"Bullshit."

Abruptly, both of their smiles dropped. The woman turned, staring coldly into her partner's eyes. He nodded and sat back up, very obviously clenching his jaw, and loosened his tie a smidge.

"Now, listen to me, you teenaged brat." Hex's already tense muscles coiled like a snake, but he didn't stop or slow. "You have two options here. You can agree to ditch the insane story about a glitching monster and keep living your insignificant life as you have been. Or you can be a stubborn idiot and wind up in juvenile detention."

Her breath caught. The man smirked, but Hex couldn't help the obvious fear that had filled her. She'd seen other kids who had come out of juvie in the system, and the stories they told were full of horror and abuse even worse than the homes.

The woman tilted her head and chimed in, "And you know how dreadfully slow the courts are these days. Who knows how long it would take for your case to be processed. Years, probably."

Hex shuddered, shoulders hunching around her neck. She couldn't go to juvie – in there, she wouldn't be able to keep track of the Creech. Wouldn't be able to figure it out, find it ... kill it. She had to stay on the outside.

So, even though it tasted sour, she said the words. "Fine. I won't talk about it anymore."

The fake smiles returned. "Excellent," the woman said as the man retrieved his briefcase and opened it on the table. "We knew you were a smart girl."

Hex scowled at her.

From the briefcase, the man produced a piece of paper and a ballpoint pen that he set down in front of Hex. It was a contract, written in legal typeface, with the tiniest font she had ever seen in her life.

"This is an agreement that stipulates that you will no longer speak of this creature to anyone," he said, holding the pen out to her. "It also rules that should you break this agreement, you will be arrested and detained until such time as a judge can rule on your case, however long that takes." His eyes, reflecting the fluorescent lights above, held a warning. So, with a shaking hand, Hex took the pen.

I don't need to talk about it, Hex thought as she signed on the dotted line. *No one believes me anyway. I can find it myself.*

The man whisked the paper and pen away, back into his briefcase, and shut it with a decisive *snick*. "There, that wasn't so difficult, was it?"

Hex shook her head and muttered, "Can I go back to class now?"

"Of course," the woman responded. "It was a pleasure to speak with you."

Hex bit her tongue to avoid saying anything snarky. The two stood up and left, just as confident as they had come in, and as the door shut behind them, the red light on the camera blinked back on.

It would take several days of research and downloading Tor, but eventually Hex managed to find a few places where people were talking about encounters like hers, and she finally had a name to fit to their bland faces.

Project Chimaera.

7

---·---

MOONLIGHT

The Creech was in the motel room.

Hex laid there, ice in her veins as the gray fog filled the room and the static filled the air. She could feel Cory beside her but dared not look. She couldn't bear to see him faceless.

It leaned over her. The shifting pattern of its scribbled skin was nauseating, but she couldn't look away. Couldn't reach for her jacket where her knife lay in the pocket at the foot of the bed. Ozone tinged her tongue.

Was this what it felt like for Mason? Were these the last few moments of her little brother, having to stare into the maw of the thing that was going to consume him?

It kept leaning closer, its strangely realistic teeth gleaming in the gray. Her mind spun off into frantic side thoughts – *why even have teeth if you don't eat flesh* – until the raising of its clawed hand snapped her back to full awareness. Maybe it was a trick of the light, but she could've sworn she saw Cory's dried blood on those claws. Cold sweat dripped down her back as the hand rose higher, higher, higher.

It plunged downwards and Hex woke with a strangled sound. She scrambled off the bed and planted her back to the wall, but when she actually opened her eyes, the room had changed. There was no fog, no gray light, no monster. Just pitch darkness, the tiny green light of the smoke detector on the ceiling, and the soft sounds Cory was making in his sleep.

Fuck. *Fuck.* Hex pressed the heels of her hands to her eyes until she saw swirling colors and held her breath. She was not going to cry over a nightmare like a little kid. She refused.

After a minute or two, the urge to cry retreated behind the veil of exhaustion. Hex dropped her hands and peered at the clock through blurry eyes; its red numbers said 3:03 a.m. She cursed under her breath.

Well, she gave it her best shot, but as usual, sleep failed her. Might as well get something done before morning.

Hex circled the bed to the side table and clicked on the lamp. Cory stirred, a sharp jerk of his head, but didn't wake.

Even in sleep he was tense: clenched jaw, balled fists, furrowed brow, all of his muscles pulled wire-taut. He jerked again, another muffled sound escaping from between gritted teeth.

Hex frowned. Some people didn't like being woken from nightmares, herself included, but –

His whole body went stiff. His nails gouged into his palms and his chest stilled as he held his breath. Before she could overthink it, Hex grabbed his shoulder and shook.

At first, he didn't react. She added a call of his name to the mix, and on the next shake his eyes flew open.

For a long moment, they stared at each other. Hex could feel him trembling, noted the way his eyes flickered as they tried to adjust to the light, and didn't move a muscle. Eventually, he blinked and let out his breath, deflating like a balloon. She waited another second before taking her hand away.

She didn't know what to say. What are you supposed to say in situations like this? After a few awkward seconds, she folded her arms over her stomach and asked, "Are you okay?"

Cory slowly levered himself upright and rolled his shoulders with an uncomfortable grimace. "Yeah. Just a nightmare. Didn't mean to wake you."

"You didn't." She rubbed her arms, bare without her jacket. "I had one too, that's what woke me up."

"Oh." He gave her a quick once-over, then asked, "Was yours about the Creech too?"

"Most of them are." Hex perched herself on the edge of the bed to dismiss the feeling of looming over him as the creature had loomed over her. "Except the one with the angry banshee. My ears still ring after that dream."

Cory mustered a chuckle. He looked more haggard than when he went to sleep, his hair spikes flattened and mussed, exhaustion heavy on his shoulders like a physical weight. "That one based on reality?"

"Oh, yeah. She shattered every window in that house."

"I don't work with ghosts much," he said, fingers picking at the duvet. There was a hint of cold sweat on his forehead. "I prefer the monsters that go away when you kill them."

It was Hex's turn to make herself laugh. "They're not too bad. Most of the time, the place isn't even haunted and I just have to sprinkle some holy water and chase the raccoons out of the attic."

"Still," Cory insisted. "The real ones are so hard to get rid of. How do you kill something that's already dead? Freaks me out."

Hex shrugged. "They are hard to get rid of, but most of the time, you don't even have to kill them. Most are just scared or confused or angry about something that happened to them. It's almost like being a therapist."

"I would be a terrible therapist," scoffed Cory, and this time Hex's laugh was genuine.

"Me too. But ghosts just make sense to me, I guess." Maybe because she had so much in common with them. Maybe because the girl Natalie had died the same day as her family, and Hex was the ghost who rose in her place, with no future ahead of her beyond *kill the thing that killed you.*

Dammit, it was too early (late? Where was the cutoff?) for her existential crises. She stood up from the bed and reached over to grab her jacket. "I'm not going to be able to go back to sleep. Want anything from the vending machine?"

Cory pushed the blankets back with a sigh. "Whatever has the most caffeine."

"You got it."

***

"Huh."

Cory raised his head from where it was resting on the table. "Huh what?" He was bleary-eyed and weary, but resolutely took another gulp of his energy drink and sat up straighter.

Hex twirled her pen over her knuckles and tapped the end of it against her notebook page. "I found the house we were in. It's a few blocks south and west of where you first saw the Creech."

"Okay," said Cory with a long blink. "Which means ...?"

"It's still trying to follow its pattern." She flipped to a different page in the notebook and spun it around to face him. Glued to the page was a basic map of the United States, cities and towns the Creech had visited marked with stars and dates, a line in red ink connecting them all with arrows indicating the direction it was taking. It was moving west, jumping from city to city, suburb to suburb, but only in the last decade had it started heading south after hitting a place in Canada. "It can't get very far hungry, but it's still trying to go in the same direction."

Cory perked up. "So we'll only have to patrol the streets to the southwest of the last house we were in."

"Exactly."

"And," he added as he leaned in to get a closer look at Hex's scribbled notes, "it only made it a few blocks last time, so it probably won't be able to make it out of the neighborhood."

Hex hummed, tapping her pen. As she had so many times before, she pondered the Creech's path. Except for once in Canada, it had stuck inside U.S. borders. Always moving west, pinballing from north to south.

"Hex? What are you thinking?"

"Nothing," she said, pushing the thought away. Cory was so practical; why should they care about why and where it was moving if that didn't matter for killing it? She leaned back, stretching her back over her chair until it popped, doggedly ignoring the sting of her cuts. "The sun will be rising soon."

Cory leaned his cheek into his hand, propped up on the table by his elbow. "We should be able to get some sleep once it comes up. My nightmares aren't as bad during the day."

"Naps are safer," Hex agreed. The words on the page before her and the satellite images of the house they'd broken into on her laptop screen blurred together, her vision going double for a moment before focusing again. Her next words slipped out by accident.

"This really sucks."

Cory snorted. "Tell me about it."

She didn't have to. The bags under Cory's eyes said he knew perfectly well all the ways that they had suffered because of this monster. Killing the Creech wouldn't bring their families back, wouldn't take the nightmares away, but at least if it was gone no one else would go through the same thing. The call and cause of every hunter that had ever lived.

One of her fingers moved idly around the trackpad on her laptop, a digital fidget, tracing the roads on the map further south, towards the edges of the neighborhood. There wasn't much there aside from the rows and rows of houses, but at the southern edge was a square of green and a symbol of a tree. *Howard Johnson Memorial Park.* Two clicks later, she was on the official city website for the park.

Hex scanned the page. She was barely absorbing any of the information, but the light and the pantomime of reading was keeping her eyes open just that little bit longer.

At the bottom of the webpage was an event calendar. There was something scheduled for that night. A high school graduation party.

Hex stared at it for a few seconds. Then she sat up straight, her heart beginning to race as she turned the screen towards Cory.

"Look," she said, jabbing a finger at the calendar. "There's a party happening in the neighborhood tonight."

Cory's eyes narrowed as he squinted at it, then widened again when he made the same connection. "A bunch of happy, successful people with good lives, all crowded together in one place."

"Like a buffet." She frowned. "But as far as we know, it's never attacked this many people at once, and usually it waits for the victims to be asleep. This doesn't fit the pattern."

"It's starving," countered Cory. "A desperate animal will do anything to survive."

"You're assuming it acts like an animal."

"And you're assuming it acts like a ghost, stuck in an infinite loop."

Hex bit the inside of her lip. Cory had a point – it clearly needed to eat, therefore it would feel the pressure of starvation – but even in this situation it was following its pattern as much as it could.

She planted her head in her hands with a frustrated groan. "God, if we could just figure out what the hell it *is*." A demon, a monster, a ghost, some cursed kid's drawing come to life?

"Is that what you were trying to do last night?" Cory's voice was almost flat, but there was a current of tension threaded through it that had Hex's muscles tensing. She raised her head to find him glaring at the surface of the table, picking at a scrape in the varnish with his fingernail.

So he was still pissed. Great.

"You could've gotten us killed, you know," he continued, still not looking up. "And those two people. Do you get that?"

Hex folded her arms over her chest, squeezing herself tight. "Of course I do."

"Then why would you – "

"Because I wanted to know. If high frequency hurt it, maybe low frequency would do something else that could be helpful."

"We knew enough." Cory's eyes finally darted up to meet Hex's, full of anger that had been simmering for hours, and she braced for whatever was going to come next. This, at least, was familiar territory. "We had it right where we wanted it. We could've killed it, right then, and all of this would be over!"

"We don't even know what kills it," Hex countered. "Bullets don't work. The frequency just seemed to stun it. What was your plan, whale on it with a bunch of different weapons until something stuck, hoping that the victims wouldn't wake up?"

"Something would've worked eventually – "

"Yeah, and that's what I was trying to figure out!"

There was a pause, a moment of quiet while they both tried to formulate their arguments, and Hex bit the inside of her cheek until it hurt. Cory was the one who invited her here, specifically because of her research and her knowledge, but now he was angry at her for exactly what he had valued her for.

"Look, if you don't want to do this, then – "

"Oh, fuck *off*." Cory shoved himself away from the table and got to his feet. Hex flinched, just the smallest bit, then curled her fingers into the biceps of her jacket and squeezed herself tighter. "What, do you think I'm here for kicks? That thing killed my mom just like it killed your family, and I am *sick* of seeing it in my fucking nightmares!"

With the anger came a rush of adrenaline that made Hex's hands tremble. There was a war in her hindbrain, seesawing between fight, flight, or freeze. This time it landed on fight.

"I don't just want to kill it, Cory," she spat back at him. She had her head tilted down to hide her eyes behind her hair, glaring at that spot on the table Cory had been picking at rather than him as he stood next to his chair, chest heaving. "I want to understand it. I want to understand why this happened to me, and to you, and to all of those other people."

"Why the hell does it matter?" asked Cory, waving his hands in the air. This time Hex didn't flinch, but she tracked those hands from her periphery.

"Because what if there are others?"

Cory paused, dropping his hands and his voice. "I thought you tracked all of its attacks."

"I did, but – I don't mean another Creech, exactly." One of her hands uncurled from the leather and began to pick at the skin around her nails. This idea had been brewing for a while, but she pushed it to the back of her mind, trying to stay focused on her real target. Now the words came pouring out. "I mean other creatures like it. Think about it. The Creech has no folklore, no origin point. It just popped up in 1924, practically out of thin air."

Cory shoved his hands into his pockets. "You don't know that," he said through gritted teeth. "Newspapers weren't as common before that, and – "

Hex couldn't help rolling her eyes. "They had newspapers for centuries before that, Cory. And I've been in libraries and archives all over the country, scouring reports from across the world, and there is no mention of it until 1924."

Out of the corner of her eye she saw Cory's mouth open, and the rest of her words came out in a rush, like a river breaking a levee.

"So, how did it get here? And, more importantly, are there other things like it that don't kill in such a distinctive way? Artificial things made of graphite and static with no origins?"

Cory mimicked her pose, crossing his arms and choosing a spot on the carpet to stare at rather than Hex's face. "It could've evolved from something else – "

"Then what? If it evolved, then it had to have an ancestor and others of its kind. So where are they?"

Cory didn't answer. He just stood there, arms folded, a battle raging on his face. Hex pressed on.

"What if this is part of Project Chimaera? What if there are more monsters out there that they're trying to cover up?"

"Okay," he said gruffly. "I get it."

Hex sat back with a shaky breath. "Listen, I am sorry for last night. It was the wrong place and the wrong time and I could've gotten us killed. I get that. But I'm not sorry for being curious."

There was a long silence. Cory stood there in deep thought, drumming his fingers against his bicep, and Hex waited in growing anxiety. This was how it always went for her, always screwing up somehow, always ending up on the outside. She wouldn't be surprised if Cory decided to go and kill the Creech on his own. Upset, but not surprised.

But when Cory met her eyes, the anger was gone, replaced by exhaustion.

"Fine. Apology accepted. Just don't do it again – I'm too young for a heart attack."

That coaxed a quiet laugh out of her, and Cory gave a tiny, tired smile. Whatever his line was, Hex hadn't gone too far over it ... yet.

With a huff, Cory let his arms drop and turned away. "Well, I'm giving up and going to sleep. You?"

"In a minute," said Hex, pulling her notebook back to her. "I want to update the chat with what we found out." And maybe start a new hypotheses list.

Apparently too tired to keep badgering her, Cory gave her a thumbs up and staggered over to the bed. He collapsed onto it face-first and let out a pained grunt when it jostled his wound.

A fond smile grew on Hex's face.

8

— · —

NEON LIGHTS

At four p.m. the dive bar was practically empty. Outside was bathed in orange afternoon light, but in the darkened interior, the neon lights hung in the windows cast bright puddles of pink and blue across the floor.

Going out had been Cory's idea (he hated being cooped up, and Hex had been able to stand his pacing for approximately an hour before breaking), but it was Hex that made them come to this place in particular – right across the road was the park the party was going to take place at.

She watched it through the window as they sat together, wound up, leg bouncing incessantly, watching for fog and straining her ears for even the faintest hint of static. This was a gamble, and if they bet wrong, they might never find the Creech again.

Cory frowned at her leg. "You're going to shake your chair apart."

"Sorry," Hex muttered, twirling a purple strand of hair around her finger. "Can't really help it."

"Do you get like this waiting for a ghost too?"

Hex shot him an unamused look, dropping her voice to a conspiratorial whisper. "No, but a ghost didn't kill my whole family."

Cory's smile was lopsided. He had redone his hair spikes before they left, now sharp enough to pop a balloon, Hex suspected. She was surprised that he carried around the extra weight of hair products, until he reminded her that he had a car and not just whatever he could fit in a single backpack.

"It could be a ghost. We don't know, remember?"

She gave him a light punch on the arm. "Smart ass."

"That's me, I'll be here all night."

"How are you so calm?" She expected another joke, another brush off, but instead, Cory's expression grew solemn.

"I'm not," he said and held out a hand. "Look." It was trembling. "Just good at pretending."

Strangely enough, Hex found that reassuring. At least she wasn't the only one freaking out.

The bartender stopped in front of them. She was pretty, with dark hair and big brown eyes. "Can I get you guys anything? You're a bit earlier than the usual crowd."

"A beer, whatever's cheapest," said Cory.

"Just soda," Hex said when the bartender's eyes turned to her. "Root beer, if you have it."

Once the bartender walked away, Cory quirked an eyebrow at her. "Don't drink?"

Hex just shook her head. She'd seen what alcohol did to people. She had no interest in being one of them.

The bartender returned with their drinks. They were both a few sips in, sitting in companionable silence as other early-comers filtered in through the doors, when a thought occurred to Hex that had her setting the drink down on the bar.

"Hey," she began, keeping her eyes glued to her fingers as she picked at her cuticles. "I just want you to know – I mean, I don't know if it's relevant, but just in case – I don't date. Or – anything. So, if this was – if you wanted – I don't."

For a second Cory stared blankly at her. Then it clicked, and for the first time since she met him, Cory looked mortified.

"No, that's not – you're nice, but I'm not really into girls."

"Not really a girl," Hex corrected, yet she smiled. The twist of anxiety in her gut (at least the one associated with Cory) unwound.

"Still. This is a strictly platonic root beer, I promise."

The front door opened. A square of orange light from the setting sun fell across Hex's face before the door closed again. They had a while before dark and the party.

A dim hum took up residence in the room as more people entered, filling up the space with idle words and the background sounds of the various sports being played on the wall-mounted TVs. Hex tapped the toes of her boots against the bar and tried to keep her nervous leg-bouncing to a minimum, going back to picking at her nails instead.

It was anticipation, yes, but there was something else that was getting to her. Something that got under her skin and made the hair on the back of her neck stand on end. She closed her eyes and listened: to their left someone was complaining about the brand of beer the bar had even as he drank it, in the back corner was a couple speaking in tense whispers, down the bar someone called for the volume of a TV to be turned up. But none of it was – there! The low, mechanical crackle of static.

Hex went cold all the way to her tapping toes and shaking fingertips.

"Cory," she whispered between her teeth after making sure the bartender was out of earshot. "Do you hear that?"

Cory paused in sipping his beer to listen. For a moment he tensed up, then glanced down the length of the bar and relaxed again.

"It's just the radio." He tipped his bottle towards the other end of the bar, where an ancient-looking radio was sitting against the wall, but Hex wasn't convinced. She knew this static, knew it in her bones, and her fears were confirmed when the bartender went over to the radio and cranked up the volume to hear the tinny weather report. And still the static buzzed in her ears.

Cory slowly set down his beer. His eyes flickered, counting off exits as he raised his hand to get the bartender's attention.

"It doesn't make any sense," he hissed, completely unnecessarily. Hex knew it didn't make sense. It was the only thought swirling in her mind. A dive bar wasn't exactly a place for the Creech's favorite snack of well-off, well-adjusted people, and they were too far from the park for the static to be this loud if it was manifesting there.

"Hey," the complaining man yelled at the bartender, "what's with the static? I can't hear the game!"

Hex pulled her backpack into her lap.

Before she could unzip it, the constant pink-blue-yellow glow of the neon lights in the windows dimmed. Cory was still trying to get the bartender's attention so that they could slip away, but his other hand rested on the bar, curled into a white-knuckled fist. From the corner of her eye Hex saw the fog leaking in through the cracks in the windows and doors.

"Cory," she murmured urgently, tasting lightning in the air. "Screw the tab, we need to go."

He dropped his arm, the hand instead diving into one of his inner pockets, probably for a weapon or his spirit box. The fog suddenly billowed across the floor, as though being blown by a stiff wind, clumping around the legs of chairs and tables.

"What's all this Halloween shit?" muttered the man at the bar as he glared down at the fog. "It's not even September."

Hex and Cory got up from their seats. Her fingers gripped the zipper of her backpack, ready to go digging for the spirit box at a moment's notice. They didn't even get that much time.

With a sudden, deafening burst of static, the lights and TVs in the bar all blinked out like extinguishing stars, filling the bar with that horrible gray light. And there, in the middle of the room, stood the Creech, its pinpoint eyes staring right at them.

There was stunned silence save the static. Then someone shouted, "What the fuck?!" and the scribbles in its skin began to shift.

Hex grabbed Cory by the lapel of his trench coat and yanked them both sideways, toppling to the floor as the Creech glitched forward. The wooden bar splintered and screams erupted from the other patrons. There were so many other people in the bar and yet the Creech turned to continue its assault, locked in on them like a heat-seeking missile.

Cory made it to his feet first and hauled Hex along with him by her wrist. Hex's head was spinning – this was so far out of pattern, they didn't have time to coordinate with spirit boxes or weapons, and it was still so focused on them, like it was –

"Hex, move!" Cory shouted in her ear, giving her a hard shove towards the door. She ran, Cory on her heels. If the Creech was so dedicated to pursuing them, the other people in the bar would be safer if they fled – right?

They burst through the front door and ran out into the parking lot. The sun was gone, the fog was thick, everything was gray, the taste of ozone in her mouth, Hex's literal worst nightmare come to life, and the plate glass window shattered as the Creech glitched through it in pursuit.

They both instinctively went for Cory's truck. Hex threw herself into the passenger seat just as the Creech glitched to where they had been standing a second before.

Cory cranked the engine, yelling over the static, "Where do we go?"

"Look for light!" Hex shouted back, then twisted around to look out the back window, scanning the flat gray for that late-afternoon orange. She found it behind one of the hedges that blocked the bar from the noise of the main road. "There!"

Hardly had the word left her lips when the passenger window exploded in a cloud of glass shards. The Creech's spindly arm was long enough to reach across the entire cab if it wanted, but instead, its claws went for Hex with lethal intent. She dove sideways, letting herself slide off the seat and into the footwell. Most of its claws slashed into the leather to reveal dense foam insulation. Pain erupted under her left cheekbone and red shone on the shortest of its claws.

"Cory! Go!"

The truck lurched into reverse. Hex smacked back into the seat, leaving a red smear, but was more interested in how the scribbles moved over the Creech's skin as it glitched away from the moving vehicle, writhing against the gray like black maggots.

She felt the impact as Cory hopped the curb and barreled through the hedges. From her position Hex couldn't see outside

– all she could do was brace her arms against the sides of the footwell and try not to hit her head.

Orange light spilled across Cory's face. The relief only lasted for a split second before bright white broke through it and Cory yanked the truck to the side, throwing Hex into the wall. A long horn sounded as Cory just barely avoided a collision.

His chest heaved. Warm blood sluiced down Hex's cheek and onto her shirt and jeans – more goddamn bloodstains for her to worry about – and she was vaguely surprised to find that even through the mad dash she still had her backpack.

"Hex?" Cory asked tersely. His eyes were glued to the windshield, his knuckles white around the steering wheel. "Are you okay?"

She took a breath. She felt fuzzy, the pain of the new cut and all the old ones filling her brain with buzzing, her fingers cold, all of her limbs shaking. But she still had her face, so, "Yeah. I'm good. I'll pay to get your seat fixed."

Cory barked out a harsh, slightly hysterical laugh. "As if that matters."

The wind whipped through the broken window. Heart rabbiting in her chest, Hex pulled herself back up onto the passenger seat, disregarding the chunky pieces of safety glass strewn all over it.

"It was hunting us." Her voice sounded distant even to her own ears.

"Looks that way," agreed Cory, mouth pressed into a grim line. He turned his head a little, just to get a glance at her, then did a double take. "Jesus, Hex, your face."

"It's nothing." She stared blankly through the windshield, brain spinning so fast it was a miracle they weren't smelling burning rubber.

The Creech recognized them. It recognized them, remembered them, followed them, and it went in for the kill, disregarding the opportunity to feed in favor of removing them as a threat.

"You were right," she murmured. "It's not just a pattern."

"That's great, I feel very vindicated." Cory slowed at the next light, glancing anxiously in the rear-view mirror. "How long do you think it would take for that thing to catch up with us?"

"I ..."

She had no idea. As far as she knew, it had never done this before. In all the cases she'd studied, if it got interrupted, the Creech would just leave, as it had the night before. She'd never seen an instance where it chased someone. How did it track them down? Was it some sort of energy they gave off that it could follow the same way it found its victims, or was it simpler than that, just following sight or sound like a wolf?

"Hex." Cory snapped his fingers. "Hello, Earth to Hex?"

"I'm thinking," she snapped back.

"What's the shortest time it's ever waited between two manifestations?" he asked. He was driving mostly legally, but pushing the upper limits of acceptable speeding. Like he feared the fog would catch up to them. For all they knew, it would.

"This is. Less than a day between last night and now."

Cory muttered a curse. "We don't know when it decided to look for us or how long it took to find us, so, worst case scenario, it's following us right now and it'll catch up as soon as we stop."

That sparked an idea. Reaching for her backpack, Hex rummaged through it until she found her radio wave detector, already tuned to the Creech's frequency. As soon as she turned it on, it began to drone.

Now it was her turn to curse.

"Any ideas, brainiac?" Cory asked.

Hex chewed on the inside of her unsliced cheek, her chest tight. "It's not acting like it's supposed to. It's never been this aggressive before."

"It's also never been this desperate before. It knows we're coming after it, so it's lashing out, like a cornered wolf."

This entire time she'd been seeing the Creech as a force of nature, like a hurricane – a hurricane didn't feel desperation when its plans were foiled, it didn't pursue certain people, it just went where the wind blew and the conditions were good. It seemed inexorable, bouncing from town to town, moving slowly year after year, decade after decade, too slow and strange to draw much attention to itself.

But it clearly had needs and, if it really was trying to kill them for being a threat, fears. If it had needs and fears, it could be manipulated. And there was one pattern it was still following.

"The fog still came," she said, slowly, like she was afraid of scaring the thought away. "The fog and the static and everything still happened. It changed when and where it manifested, but it couldn't change how."

"So we'll know when it's coming." A sharp, wolfish grin spread across Cory's face. "We can trap it."

9

HEADLIGHTS

They drove out of town, into the rolling hills that surrounded the city. The air was cool and humid, streaming in through the shattered truck window, blowing Hex's hair back as they searched for a suitable place to lay their trap.

They found it soon enough – an open field of green grass, surrounded by sparse woods. Cory pulled off the road and trundled a few feet into the clearing, the truck jarring and jostling. All the way, the radio wave detector in Hex's lap kept up a soft drone.

They had worked out a plan on the way over. Now all there was left to do was put it in motion.

Cory parked a short distance from the road. He left the headlights on, beaming out into the trees on the other side of the clearing, casting long, deep shadows.

Hex's hands were shaking as she dug out her supplies. Spirit box, flashlight, the humming frequency detector. Cory, handing over his own spirit box, noticed.

"Do you want to be the one in here? I can – "

"No," said Hex, tightening her grip on the little radios. "I want to do this."

To her relief, Cory didn't fight her on it. He just nodded and methodically began loading his pistol to have at the ready. Bullets wouldn't kill the Creech, but they could at least be distracting.

With a final, bracing breath, Hex peeled her jacket from her shoulders. "Look after this for me?"

Her life was one thing, but she wasn't about to risk her most precious possession to the Creech's claws. Cory nodded, hard determination in his eyes.

Hex tossed it into the backseat, where hopefully it would be safe, then before she could think twice about it, climbed out of the truck. Her boots sunk into the soft grass, like it was trying to stop her, hold her in place. The cicadas in the trees were deafening, the crickets loud in her ears, and the dried blood running down her cheek cracked into flakes with every motion of her jaw.

She strode forward and took up a position on the edge of the light, flittering with little insects revealed by and drawn to the beams, turning the spirit boxes as high as they could go. The last of the sun disappeared behind the hills and the moon shone down silver, sliced through by the artificial beams of the headlights.

Cory sat in the truck with the driver's side door open, just as tense as Hex as the minutes passed, the frequency detector trilling louder and louder. She was prepared to wait as long as she had to – ghost hunts were an exercise in pointless patience – but it didn't take long before the lights on the detector were flashing red.

Hex switched it off and let it fall to the grass next to her feet. She kept her shaking legs braced, a spirit box in each hand, thumbs poised over the buttons. The timing had to be perfect. Too soon and the Creech might call off the attack and vanish again. Too late and ...

Fog spilled out from between the trees. It crawled across the grass like malignant hands, grasping at blades of grass to haul itself forward, and the silver light of the moon began to shift into dull gray. It reached Hex's feet, swirled thick around her ankles, and still she kept herself in the same spot. The consuming fear that had devoured her before was nowhere to be found. In its place was determination, braced by the chill of adrenaline in her veins and the taste of ozone on her tongue.

The shadows had vanished with the gray light, making it easier to see the movement behind one of the trees. Familiar, jerking movement that vanished and reappeared behind another tree.

For a second she went back – rough bark against her palms, the stitch burning in her side, the monster jumping from tree to tree as it stalked her – until she latched onto the dim, washed-out glow of the truck's headlights and hauled herself back to reality, just in time for the Creech to glitch into existence before her.

She didn't freeze. She didn't hesitate. The Creech came in swinging and Hex ducked under its arm, jamming her thumb against the power button on her spirit box. The sound that came out was painfully high-pitched and loud enough to send any dogs within five hundred yards running.

The Creech's body jerked, the scribbles on its skin writhing. Silently, it raised its clawed hands again, but Hex was already dropping the spirit box to the ground and diving under its next strike. She stumbled, one knee hitting the ground before the momentum carried her another few staggering steps.

A sharp *crack* rang through the clearing, and the Creech made a sound like nails on a chalkboard. Cory, giving her time to get to the second spot.

She made it there on her knees, slammed the button on the second spirit box, and let it fall to the grass. When she looked up, the Creech was standing over her, the markings on its skin practically vibrating, the edges of its form jolting and jittering like it was trying to move and couldn't, and Hex's hands shook with hope.

The plan was working.

The Creech vanished for a split second and came back facing the truck, and Hex cried out to Cory over the cacophony of static.

"Turn it on!"

Cory hopped back into the driver's seat. Even more noise came pouring from the vehicle as he cranked the volume, the radio set to the same frequency as the spirit boxes.

The Creech's body blurred with the speed at which it was trying and failing to get away. A low groan reverberated out from it, in stark contrast to all the shrieking radios – the ominous creak of metal slowly giving way to great pressure. Leaving the spirit box in the grass, Hex pushed herself back and out of range of the claws, then staggered to her feet. She couldn't believe it – it actually worked!

Then the Creech reached out with its long arms, its movement stuttering like a storyboard sketch, and with surgical precision, smashed the second spirit box to pieces with its claws.

Time seemed to stand still as the sound cut out in the broken box. Those pinpoint eyes locked on Hex, who stared back with her heart threatening to choke her.

Of course, said the little voice at the back of her mind as she stood there, her boots glued to the ground. *If it's smart enough to hunt, it's smart enough to break something it doesn't like. Stupid, stupid –*

Crack!

The Creech jerked and Hex's head snapped around. Cory was standing in the headlights, the only thing casting a shadow in the gray void, the barrel of his gun trained on the Creech. He pulled the trigger again, making Hex nearly jump out of her skin, before the Creech let out a metallic grinding sound and glitched ten feet closer to Cory.

Nauseating adrenaline suddenly ignited into fury. The image of Mason, helpless in the monster's grip, burned away the fear keeping her feet pinned.

She wasn't going to lose anyone else.

It took only a few seconds to close the distance. The blade of her knife tore into its scribbled skin with a sound like ripping paper. There was no resistance to its flesh; the knife went through it so easily, tearing a ragged wound clear across the Creech's back. And on the inside there was ... nothing. It was hollow.

The Creech's huge hand slammed into her side, knocking Hex to the ground with a hard *thunk*. Pain radiated from her ribs in a starburst and she couldn't tell if it was from the impact with the hand or the ground, but what did it matter? It was looming over her with that grin full of wolf's teeth and for a moment she was frozen, just like in her dream.

There was a dim shout, muffled by the ringing in Hex's ears and the fog that sat so thick in the air and in her throat. Then, with a flash of green and orange, Cory threw himself bodily into the Creech.

It almost seemed like it would topple over. At the last second it went incorporeal, letting Cory hit the ground and roll, before reappearing over him with a burst of static.

It looked so much like it had that day in Mason's bedroom, all bent over, skin squirming like it was alive, leaning down closer for its meal. She could've lost herself again if it weren't for the pain: in her side, on her back, on her face, in her knuckles where she gripped her knife like it was welded to her skin.

Hex grabbed a fistful of grass and hauled herself upright.

Cory, ever prepared, twisted until he could pull a slender blade of his own from one of his pockets and plunge it into the Creech's side. It tore the skin just like Hex's knife had, and the creaking groan returned as Cory slashed at it again and again. The back of Hex's shirt was soaked with dew and cold sweat.

In three steps she was behind it. It saw her coming this time and vanished.

She spun around just in time to duck beneath its claws. The wounds Cory had left across its abdomen were already knitting themselves closed again as it had with the bullets, but through the connecting strands, she still saw nothing but air and the white of its skin on the other side. Like a monster made of paper mâché, some kid's Halloween craft project gone wrong. So terribly, terribly wrong.

"Stay down!" Cory shouted. A second later Cory's knife spun over her head, aimed at the Creech's chest. She expected it to tear right through and keep going, but to both of their surprise, the blade struck something and ricocheted off, a dim sound like a ringing bell reverberating from the strike.

This was her chance. Hex sprang upwards, aiming her knife at the same spot. It went through the skin just as easily as before, only to stop with a jarring impact she felt all the way up her arm.

The Creech froze. Its expression didn't change, but Hex imagined she could see shock in the squirming lines of its body.

Bracing her other hand on the hilt, Hex slowly twisted the blade around the obstruction, carving through scant paper resistance. And the Creech just stood there, craned over her as if in a trance, with a new sound spilling out of its hollow throat – a long, low keen, crackling in a staticky death-rattle. The fog flickered, and Hex glimpsed stars overhead.

With one final burst of strength, she wrenched the metal object from the Creech's chest. It thudded into the grass at her feet, leaving behind a gaping hole with black edges. Edges that were rapidly spreading.

Hex and the Creech both stared at each other as the black spread like spilled ink on paper, climbing and branching through the fibers of skin, engulfing its signature squiggle marks that, for the first time, were perfectly still. The dark spread down its arms and coated its claws, up its neck and over its teeth, its eyes vanishing under its onslaught, all while it stood there, unmoving. For a moment it stood, a stark black statue against the gray light.

Then the Creech folded in on itself like a house of cards. The black particles fell around her, leaving black smears on the backs of her hands and her bare arms. The gray light faded and fell away.

The monster was gone.

10

— • —

SUNLIGHT

Unmuffled by the fog, Cory's ecstatic whoop rang across the clearing. "We did it!" he cried, throwing his arms into the air. "We killed it! We actually *fucking killed it*!" He spun in a circle, his trench coat flaring out and raining stray pieces of grass, and when that wasn't enough, took off at a sprint, cheering all the way.

Hex didn't move an inch. She stared down at the pile of dust, the buzzing in her skull even louder than the truck radio and the remaining spirit box somewhere in the grass. She half expected the pile to start moving, to piece itself back together and call the fog back, but everything was still. Goosebumps pricked up her bare arms. The stillness was almost worse.

The shine of the headlights caught something in the grass between her feet. Slowly, smothering winces at the pain that was making itself known as the adrenaline faded, she knelt down to retrieve it.

It was the thing that she carved out of the Creech's chest.

She stood up, turning it over in her hands. It was about the size of her palm, made of cool metal with tiny dents and divots. When she held it up to the headlights, its shape became clear: it was a little metal heart, imperfectly cast and covered in rust. Hex could feel the questions rising, held back only by the fog of pain and broken dissociation, but before she could fall down the rabbit hole, Cory came sprinting back up to her, a wild grin on his face.

"We did it!" he cheered again, and threw his arms around her. He probably would've picked her up and spun her around if she hadn't let out a choked cry.

Immediately he let go and stepped back, his expression flipping to concern in less than a second. "What's wrong? Are you hurt?" One hand was still on her shoulder. Hex reached up and grasped his wrist while she tried to get her breath back enough to answer, the metal heart secure in her other hand.

"Ribs. Might be broken."

"Shit, sorry," Cory hissed. "How's your breathing? Can you talk?"

"Y-yeah, I can breathe, just hurts."

"Okay, here. Let's get back to the truck."

"Wait," she said, balking, staring at the pile of ashes. "What if it's not dead? What if it regenerates or something – "

"Hex. It's a pile of dust."

"Still – !"

Cory turned and put his other hand on her shoulder, making her meet his solemn, firm eyes.

"Listen to me. You're holding its heart in your hand." He smiled again, blindingly bright, and if Hex wasn't mistaken there were tears in his eyes. "You avenged them. *All* of them."

Her little brother's face flashed through her mind. Her parents' bed, occupied by empty clothes. Suddenly, she felt like crying too, and before she could stop them, the tears fell, leaving warm trails in their wake and stinging across the slice on her cheek.

"We did," she managed to croak out.

Cory made a sympathetic sound and squeezed her shoulder. "Come on. Let's get out of here."

***

The diner was on the edge of the city, one of those classic places trying to emulate a time long past, open 24/7. Bandaged and bedraggled as they were, they surprisingly didn't get any comments from the waitress when she directed them to a booth next to a window. All she said was, "I'll be quick with that coffee," and winked before rushing back to the kitchen.

Thankfully, Hex's ribs were bruised, not broken. If they were broken, she would've had to go to the hospital and answer too many questions. As it was, she just ached, the fresh bandage on her cheek pulling when she moved her jaw. Maybe she could bum a couple more painkillers off of Cory before she moved on.

That thought made her stomach twist, but she resolutely ignored the quiet dread beginning to form. Having someone around had been nice, especially when she didn't need to watch what she said around them as far as hunting went, but she always knew it wasn't going to last. Cory needed her to hunt the Creech and that was it. An alliance of convenience.

"Here we are." The waitress had reappeared with a full coffee pot and filled their cups generously. "What can I get ya?"

Cory ordered a mountain of pancakes. Hex went for French toast and downed two cups of coffee before the food even made it to the table. Neither of them said a word as they ate, but Hex's brain never slowed down.

She still had questions that needed answering, a few hypotheses to chase, but first she needed to go back to her regular hunting – this little sabbatical had put a serious dent in her meager funds. Maybe she could convince Cory to drop her off at the nearest bus stop, or even better, a truck stop. Her hair could use a wash, and she had black smears of Creech dust on her hands like charcoal.

Once the food was gone, Hex's hand found its way back to the metal heart. She held it under the table, memorizing every dent and streak of rust. Somewhere under the buzz of bottomless coffee and barely-held-back dissociation, there was a hint of frustration – *they'd finally killed the damn thing and still it left more questions* – but she passed it back and forth between her hands, unable to let it go.

Cory was the picture of contentment as he sipped his coffee, watching the cars rush by and the stars slowly retreat from the dawn threatening the horizon. His fingers tapped against the table, probably eager to get back on the road, back to life now that it was all over.

Hex felt staticky. Too many emotions crackling under her skin.

With a little shake of his head, Cory opened his mouth. "Hey, I've been thinking – "

Something buzzed. Cory made an annoyed sound and dug his phone out of his pocket. His glare faltered when he saw the caller ID.

"Sorry, I should probably answer this." He slid out of the booth and headed for the front door. Hex kept watching the dawn.

She needed to get a grip. The sleep deprivation probably wasn't helping. She rubbed her eyes, scrubbed her hand over her face, bringing the smell of the rusted metal heart with it.

Cory came into view, pacing the length of the diner as he talked. He smiled at something the person on the other end said, then laughed.

Hex was perfectly happy being on her own. She'd been alone for a long time and she was used to it. It shouldn't be hard for her to say goodbye to Cory and hop on the next bus to wherever another ghost (or family of raccoons) was plaguing someone's home.

So why did the thought of parting make her throat tighten?

She sighed and tucked the metal heart into her pocket. Cory was so happy that the Creech was dead – he probably wouldn't want her around if she was going to keep going after the mystery. Like he said back in the hotel room, he just wanted it to be over, and it was. So they were too. She looked away, plastering a neutral expression on her face, and started looking up bus routes on her phone.

Eventually, Cory came back to the booth. Hex didn't ask, just glanced at him, but he answered the unspoken question. "It was a friend of mine who lives in Southern Texas. He was saying that he'd heard rumors about a neighborhood having a chupacabra problem."

Hex snorted. "Classic Texas."

"Yeah," agreed Cory, but his eyes were serious when he looked up. "He also said his daughter saw a ghost walking around in the desert. Scared the crap out of her."

She swallowed, fighting to keep her tone light. "Sounds pretty serious."

Don't get your hopes up.

"It's kind of perfect, because I was thinking" – Cory fiddled with a tiny plastic container of creamer, rolling it back and forth across the table – "maybe we could stick together for a while?

I mean, we worked pretty well together, and I think we could both stand to diversify, so to speak, and that way we could get more jobs, and you wouldn't have to take buses everywhere. So, you know, just a thought."

The static calmed, and a smile grew over Hex's lips.

"I'd love to."

Cory let out the breath he'd been holding. "Thank God. I don't think I could stand singing Bon Jovi to myself for another road trip."

That pulled a laugh out of her. "Don't worry. I have plenty of recommendations that were written this century." Relief was light in her stomach like helium, and Cory looked at her with shining eyes. The life of a hunter was such a lonely one, after all. Maybe Hex wasn't the only one who felt it.

"So, partners then?" he asked, offering a fist across the table. Hex bumped it with her own.

"Partners."

ACKNOWLEDGEMENTS

I owe my sincere gratitude to my friends, Athena and Alika. Without Athena's help this book would not exist, and without Alika, neither would Hex.

About the Author

Jayde Layne is an ASU graduate, now living in Flagstaff, Arizona. Her work focuses on horror and dark fiction.

— • —

Before You Go

This is the second book in 12 Months of Whump, a series of whumpy novellas published by WPP throughout 2025. Each novella can be read as a standalone.

To stay up to date with the 12 Months of Whump series and other whumperfly-inducing projects, visit us at https://thewhumpyprintingpress.tumblr.com/